XUL

CAPTURED BY ALIENS: BOOK ONE

A.G. WILDE

Xul

Xul © A. G. Wilde 2019

All rights reserved. No part of this book may be used or reproduced in any manner whatsoever without written permission except in the case of brief quotations embodied in critical articles or reviews.

The characters and events portrayed in this book are fictitious. Any similarity to real persons, living or dead, businesses, or locales is coincidental and is not intended by the author.

This book is dedicated to that girl who is trying new things.
Keep on trying.

DISCLAIMER

This work of fiction is intended for mature audiences only.

All sexually active characters portrayed in this book are eighteen years of age or older.

XUL

Athena wakes up in hell.

Well...it's an alien slave ship, but it might as well be hell because she only has three choices.

Mate. Become a sex slave. Or be killed.

Great options.

Desperate for freedom, a chance for survival is presented in the handsome rogue alien called Xul.

But Xul is caught up in problems of his own and a mission he cannot afford to let fail—one that could be easily compromised if he dared open his heart.

That doesn't leave her with many options and it doesn't help that she finds him utterly frustrating...

...and strong, hot, irresistible...

She shouldn't really be thinking about him like that. Should she?

Xul is a standalone read that contains delightfully steamy scenes with a guaranteed happily ever after, possessive alpha males, and strong female leads. There is no forced mating between the hero and heroine and no cliffhanger. It is the first book in the Captured by Aliens sci-fi alien romance series.

FOREWORD

Athena and Xul's story starts off rough with some harsh scenes (not between the two of them)—but keep on reading. It gets better. I promise <3.

1

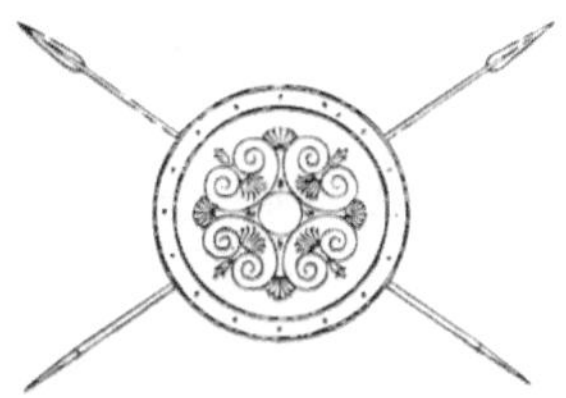

They say two things happen when you die.

One: You stop breathing.

That one was obvious.

Two: Your soul leaves your body to go to its final resting place.

Wherever that was.

As her eyes opened to the dim blue lights above her, Athena knew one thing for sure: her soul must be lost because there was no way this was her final resting place.

She didn't mind dying. Dying was a part of having been given the gift of "living." However, if this was what the afterlife looked like, she needed to have a word with whoever was in charge.

Eyes opening a little further, she realized the dim blue light wasn't just emanating from above her head; it surrounded the entire room, yet she could see no light bulbs or any indication as to where the light was coming from.

"Well, what do you know...Satan has some high-tech shit," she murmured. Her voice was soft as she spoke and it seemed to disappear into the room as if the walls were padded.

Groaning as her eyes opened a little further, she tried to lift her neck and a sharp pain shot down her spine.

Oh yes, she remembered now.

That sharp pain.

It was the last thing in her memory, actually.

The strange sound in the backyard.

Opening the back door to investigate if her pet dog, Magnet, had gotten himself stuck in the fence again.

Stepping onto the porch.

Hearing another sound.

The sharp pain in the back of her neck.

The world going black.

It hadn't occurred to her that she had any enemies, but the last thought that had left her mind was, "Fuck, I've been shot."

Yet, now, as she reached her hand to the back of her neck to feel the wound, a chill ran down her spine.

There was something metal there.

Cold and metal.

That was enough to wake her up and Athena's eyes flew wide open as she grabbed at the thing at the back of her neck.

It was long and it extended for as far as her hand could stretch. It was fastened somehow, deep into her skin, and the longer she held on to it, the more she could feel the rhythmic pulse echoing through the metal.

"What the hell?"

It was only when she tried to get up that she realized her legs were bound to whatever slab she was lying on.

As she struggled to release herself, the dim lights suddenly changed to amber and she could finally see the room a bit more clearly, though visibility was still low.

But it wasn't a room.

It was a cell.

And her legs, they were bound by chains.

But that wasn't the only alarming thing. Her skin bristled as she realized she was stark naked.

What in the world?

A grunt by the cell wall made her turn her head sharply to the presence that suddenly stood there.

Burning green eyes stared back at her as the cell opened and a beast of a man walked in, his footsteps so heavy she could feel the ground vibrate under his weight.

He was carrying what she could only surmise was a weapon, a spear-like rod that glinted in the light.

"Where am I?" Athena asked, her eyes wild. "What are you going to do to me?"

The man said nothing. Instead, he went and stood by the wall, taking the stance of a guard as he placed the spear in front of him.

"Where am I?!" she asked again, her voice rising.

The man said nothing and what she could only describe as a snort of hot air blew from his nostrils.

As her eyes cleared, Athena gulped.

She must be dreaming.

Shaking her head as if that would clear her thoughts, she stared at the man by the wall, her eyes widening with each second that it took her brain to process what she was seeing.

He was big alright, his muscles well-defined.

He was wearing nothing but a loincloth that covered his...um, area...and a glowing golden ring that hung from his nose. Not quite the wardrobe she'd have chosen but to each his own.

From his head grew a long brown mane and piercing through the mane up into the air were his two...Athena's eyes widened some more...horns?

HORNS?!

Wait...this was no man...

Judging from those horns, it was the devil himself.

The mother-freakin-devil.

So she did end up in hell.

Well, how about that? Her good-for-nothing mother had been right all along. All those years of calling her a 'demon-child' had actually rung true.

But, before she had time to process what she was seeing fully, a glowing light entered the room.

It was a light-blue ring that hovered above the ground. A form of transport, she supposed, because something was riding on top of it.

Her entire being froze as her brain refused to comprehend what she was seeing.

If the pain in her neck wasn't any indication, then the sudden rush of her heartbeat in her ears was enough to tell her one thing: she was alive.

And if she was alive, this wasn't hell...but it definitely wasn't heaven either.

And maybe, it wasn't even Earth.

The world fell black again as she fainted.

THE PAIN in her neck was intense and whatever was prodding her was doing so mercilessly, poking something hard into her ribs and grunting.

"Do' li liduk, doraba."

Athena's eyes flew open.

Blue-lit room.

Legs chained.

Tall man-devil-bull thing.

Other thing hovering on a light-blue ring above the floor.

She hadn't been dreaming.

Struggling to sit upright, she was sharply pushed back down by the butt of the devil's spear-like weapon.

"Do' fahevbekraba mefa."

It was speaking. Maybe to her or maybe to the other thing beside it, which was moving towards her, slowly hovering on its light-blue ring.

She could see it clearer now and it was hideous. Its skin was wrinkly and moist, with some kind of ooze seeping from it. Its two eyes protruded on stalks high above its head and it had some kind of purple fluorescent spots along its back.

"Stay away from me!" Athena tried to scramble backward but there wasn't much place for her to go, especially with her legs still chained and whatever was attached to her neck still holding her in place.

To her horror, the thing raised what looked like some sort of gun and pointed it towards her as it approached.

"No, don't! What do you want?!" Athena struggled against the chains but they wouldn't budge. "Stay away from me!"

She was shouting at the top of her voice, but as before, the sounds emanating from her mouth seemed to just be soaked up by the room.

"Tee ed jsued," the thing said, ooze seeping from its mouth, which suddenly appeared as it spoke.

It wasn't listening to her. It didn't seem to care.

In those two protruding eyes, she saw not one sliver of emotion.

This was it.

She was going to be shot by some glorified slug.

This was how she was going to die.

The devil moved over to her in the next instant, grasping her shoulders with his strong hands and rendering her unable to squirm or move away.

"Let go of me!" She flailed her legs, trying to release herself from his grasp but she couldn't do it. He was too strong. Much too powerful, and she was very aware that if he wanted to, he could snap her shoulders without even exerting any effort.

The cool metal of the gun behind her ear was the next thing she felt and, in the next instant, there was a sharp pain that lasted only a second.

"Translator. Administered," the slug said, and she was released by the devil, causing her to fall back suddenly.

Athena blinked wildly, her body still trembling, as she realized she could understand what they were saying.

"Gender test. Next," the slug said, moving around to her legs.

Athena's eyes widened.

Gender test? Did that mean they were going to…?

Oh, hell no.

The devil moved around to her legs then and Athena tried to wriggle away but the chains held her fast.

"Open your legs," the devil said.

"Like hell I will!" Athena kicked at the chains and struggled, but with the metal tube attached to her neck holding her in place, there wasn't much she could do.

She didn't know where the hell she was but she wasn't about to just let them do what they wanted.

If this was how she was going to die, she was not going to make it easy for them. She would not comply.

A short snort left the devil's nose and she locked her fiery eyes with his.

Was that amusement she saw in his green orbs?

She wasn't sure.

What did the devil look like when he was amused?

"I'm sure it's female," he said, his eyes still locked with hers but it seemed as if he was speaking to the slug.

"The checks. Must be done," the slug replied. When it wasn't speaking, it looked as if it had no mouth, but as soon as it started to speak, a thin line would appear on its face and the words would come out.

It was downright disturbing, but she didn't have time to think about that because her legs were suddenly being moved.

Grasping her ankles, the devil forcefully spread her legs, opening her so her nakedness was fully exposed to them.

He held her legs fast, so she was no longer able to move them, and the slug approached.

"Don't! Don't you fucking dare you—you slimy, boneless piece of shit!" Athena snarled at him and the slug paused.

"I am not. A piece. Of shit," it said. "I am an Isclit. From the great Iscli—"

"You could be Captain Fucking America, for all I care. Don't you put your slimy hands on me!" Athena glared at the slug.

In the corner of her eye, she saw what looked like a hint of a smile pass over the devil's face.

The Isclit looked at her, its eyes still showing no emotion, then from somewhere in its body, what she could only describe as a remote protruded from through a hole that suddenly appeared through its ooze.

The devil snorted, his gaze narrowing and becoming murderous, as his large hands tightened around her ankles. It was as if he was trying to prevent himself from doing something and it only made Athena more alarmed.

Whatever that remote was, it wasn't goo—

It was immediate, the pain. She couldn't describe what it was or how it was happening to her, all Athena knew was that her entire body was in excruciating pain. It made her body stiffen and her back arch as it seemed to come from every nerve ending under her skin. Tears sprung in her eyes as her mouth opened and she gasped for air.

She was dying, but what was killing her?

The pain seemed to be coming from within her body, not outside of it.

And then, at the point she felt was the end, the pain suddenly eased and she fell back. Her heart was racing and, as her vision cleared, she noticed the Isclit move its finger off a button on the remote.

Whatever had just happened to her, it had caused it. It had somehow controlled her pain using the remote.

"What the hell did you just do to me?!" Athena spoke through gritted teeth.

"You will. Comply," the slug said. "Or. You will. Be Punished."

Her chest was rising and falling in quick succession now, as her heart was beating as if it wanted to pop out of her chest along with her lungs. She had found herself in sticky situations before, but this one...how was she supposed to escape from this?

In the next instant, she was spun on her belly, her feet twisting in the chains, and her legs forced underneath her so she was kneeling with her ass in the air.

"Gender. Test," the Isclit said and Athena growled.

The next thing she felt made her scream, not in pain, but from the sheer thought that the thing that touched her privates was some appendage of the Isclit. She knew it was because there was only one being in the room whose body oozed goo and at that moment, she could feel the goo dripping down her legs.

The appendage felt like a soft, wet hand that had suction. Athena tried to pull herself away, but she was still being held by the devil.

The wet, oozy appendage covered her fully, feeling between her lips and clit as it spread her folds and moved over every inch of her.

"Fuck! You sick bastard!"

Just then, the appendage left her body and she was spun to rest on her back again.

"Gender confirmed. Female," the Isclit said, turning on its light-blue ring as it began to move toward the cell door.

"You could have just asked, you pervert!"

This time she was sure of it; apparently, the devil was amused. But she didn't have time to think about him. At the moment, he was not the more obnoxious of the two beings holding her captive.

The Isclit was.

"You have a remote that can bring pain but no technology to tell the gender of people you kidnap? Not as smart as you think you are," Athena spoke through gritted teeth.

As she finished, the Isclit paused his movement and turned to look at her again. Eyes still without emotion, the remote emerged from his body.

Athena's eyes widened. She knew what was coming but this time, when the pain hit her, she was ready for it.

It shot through her body like a raging fire and her blood was the kerosene it fed on. It knocked the wind out of her, causing her to stiffen again as she inhaled deeply.

With gritted teeth, she glared at the Isclit as the pain threatened to tear her apart from the insides. Her eyes watered and she couldn't breathe.

Then the Isclit stopped pushing the button and the pain ceased.

"You will. Comply," it said.

Athena fell back against the slab and a short chuckle left her lips. "I bet you wouldn't be so bad if I had a bag of salt."

The Isclit blinked at her and she realized it didn't understand what she meant. That was probably for the best.

If it did understand, it may have decided to push its torture button again and she wasn't sure she could handle that level of pain in such a short interval.

"Take her to the terrarium."

Athena's eyes flew to the devil just in time to see him nod.

Terrarium?

2

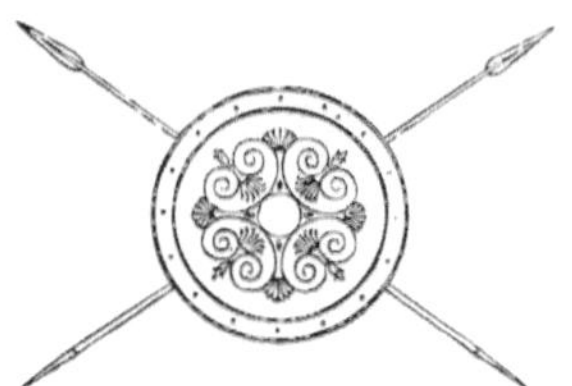

As the Isclit exited the cell, Athena noticed that the door shifted to let the creature through before settling back into place with no evident indication a door was ever there. It looked like all bars. She was surprised she didn't notice that before.

If she was going to get out of this place, she needed to pay more attention to the little things. She'd have to keep a keen eye on everything that occurred around her.

At the sound of moving chains, she swiveled her head around to stare at the devil. He undid the locks on her ankle cuffs and the chains dropped to the floor with a clank.

Athena pulled her legs up towards herself and scuttled away from him, eyeing him as he stepped towards her.

"Stay away," she warned, but the devil didn't stop moving.

"I said, stay away!" Her back was against the wall now and there was nowhere to go. Glancing quickly around the cell, she searched for a weapon and her eyes landed on the discarded chains on the floor.

Could she reach them in time?

If she could get to them, maybe she could use them as a weapon to defend herself.

The devil snorted as he realized what she was looking at.

"Don't even think about it," he said, as he came to stand over her.

Sneering at him, Athena narrowed her eyes.

The devil leaned forward and Athena's breath caught in her throat the nearer he came.

He was much bigger than she'd initially realized. He practically dwarfed her.

And he was...handsome? With his head so close, she could see that he had a chiseled face with a strong jaw, a flattened nose that had a large gold ring piercing between his nostrils, and deep green eyes that were staring straight back at her.

"Be still," he said, and Athena found she couldn't move.

The devil reached behind her neck and, in the next moment, he brushed her golden hair out of the way and the metal tube in her neck was detached.

"The Supplicator has been detached," he said, easing away.

She assumed he was speaking about the metal tube and she reached her hand to touch the back of her neck, expecting a gaping hole to be there.

Instead, there was nothing. No wound. No holes. Nothing.

It was as if the metal tube hadn't been attached to her at all.

For a second, she almost forgot the devil was standing there, till he reached for her and she jumped and scrambled across the cell.

He paused, his green eyes tracking her every movement.

The thought that she was naked and alone in God-knows-where didn't help the fact that she had this...beast...watching her like she was his prey and he a hunter. However, instead of pulling out some remote from his nether regions, he just narrowed his eyes as he watched her move.

He was different from the Isclit, she noticed. Not so intent on hurting her as the slug was.

"We must move. There isn't much time," he said.

"Where are you taking me?"

"To the terrarium where you will be placed for viewing," he answered, as he reached for his weapon. The metal on the edge of the spear looked sharp and she wondered if he was going to use it against her to follow his commands.

Instead, he held the spear at his side.

"It would be best if you do as I say. The Isclit will return and I am not in the mood for pain because of your stubbornness." He stepped toward her, moving so fast she didn't have time to run.

Her brain went on autopilot and she grabbed for the chains, swinging them in his direction.

The chains hit his chest, without so much as leaving a mark, before falling to the floor.

Holding firmly onto her arm, he jerked her towards him and a soft yelp escaped her lips.

The sound seemed to catch him off guard and his brows furrowed.

"Come." He seemed to gather himself quickly and jerked her toward the cell door. "Do not resist. Resisting brings pain, and," he paused, his green eyes roving over her nakedness, "your species doesn't look like it can handle much pain."

She was about to protest when the cell door opened and the devil pulled her into a long brightly lit hallway with what looked like cells lining the entire length of it on either side.

"Dammit," Athena cursed underneath her breath. She hadn't seen how he'd opened the cell. She'd have to pay better attention next time.

It was strange the light was so bright in the hallway yet none of the brightness seeped into the cells. No sounds came from the cells either, yet, as the devil pulled her along, Athena saw outlines of various forms inside, including Isclits and soldiers.

Glancing up at him now in the bright light, her eyes widened a little as she was able to see him clearly.

His body was coated in a layer of brown fuzz, and she hadn't been mistaken when she'd realized he was handsome.

It was weird.

He was definitely not a man, definitely not human, but he was obviously male, a powerful one, and something about his face made him attractive.

But the ring in his nose and the horns protruding from his head reminded her of a bull.

Was that what he was? A bull-man?

And she thought he was handsome?

If she got out of this, she would have to seriously reconsider her taste in men...that, and she'd probably never be able to eat beef ever again.

His grip on her arm was firm and Athena glared up at him as she tried to yank her arm away, elbowing him in the side in the process. The devil glanced down at her and she saw that amused look cross his face again, as if her attempts were futile.

He did call her frail before. Well, she'd show him. She was stronger than she looked.

"Be still, or I will have to restrain you." He glanced down at her. "You do not want that."

Athena's brows furrowed slightly as the implication of his words sunk into her. Restrained? He was supposed to restrain her but he hadn't. Why not?

Before she could mull it over, another guard rounded the corner and Athena gasped. It was tall with a long snout with jagged teeth protruding over the edges—teeth she was sure were used for ripping its prey to pieces. Its skin was hard and leathery and it had a long tail that whipped behind it.

As it caught her gaze, its yellow eyes locked on her and it dipped its head towards her and snarled, causing Athena to jump back in fright.

The beast threw its head back and laughed before continuing on its way.

Behind it, with a heavy chain around its neck, was what looked like a human male. The man looked to be in his fifties and he was as stark naked as she was.

"Move!" the beast snarled again, pulling hard on the chain,

causing the man to stumble. With a roar, the beast brandished a whip and with a crack, the whip landed on the man's back.

Athena winced as the man cried out in pain.

"Stand!" the beast ordered and the man got shakily to his feet, the chain around his neck pulling him forward as the beast continued on its way.

Athena's eyes widened as she looked up at the devil.

Was that what he'd meant by restraining her?

"I assume that is the male of your species," the devil murmured, as he continued walking. Her legs complied on their own, as Athena found she had suddenly gone weak in the knees.

What was this place?

Where the hell was she?

"Feeble, just like the females," the devil continued.

Athena ignored him, instead opting to ask a question of her own. If he was in the mood for speaking, maybe she could get some information to help her when she finally got a chance to escape.

"Where are they taking him? Is he going to a terrarium?"

"No," the devil answered. "The males of the species are often disposed of, if they are not used for mating."

"Disposed of?"

"Killed. Their bodies ground to make bites."

Whatever was left in her stomach from her last meal threatened to rise to her throat.

Just then, another guard walked past them. Behind him, another older man on a chain was being yanked along. On his back were deep welts where a whip must have landed.

Athena gulped, her eyes darting to the large hand that was grasping her arm.

Why hadn't he restrained her?

Just then, they stopped walking and Athena realized they were standing in front of a large wall.

In the next second, a door appeared on the flat surface and they were let into a large dim room. Athena frowned. She still hadn't managed to see how he'd opened the door. Where were these hidden doors and how was he managing to open them?

In the center of the room was a brightly lit area surrounded by glass. From what she could see, it looked as if there was a forest behind the glass.

"You." The voice came out of nowhere and made her jump. Turning her head to the side, she noticed a light-blue ring coming towards them through the darkness. On top of it was an Isclit and the immediate memory of the pain she'd felt in the cell came flooding back.

"Why is this. Human. Not restrained?"

"The human is compliant," the devil said.

Athena glanced up at the devil, but he was not looking at her. Compliant? After she'd seen a man getting whipped for just stumbling, she was surprised he hadn't done the same to her for throwing the chain at him and trying to yank her arm away as he'd carried her through the hall.

What was he up to?

"Good," the Isclit said, moving the hovercraft over to her. "Put it in. The terrarium. For viewing."

As the devil pulled her toward the brightly lit forest, she realized it must be a different Isclit. This one had green fluorescent spots on its back. The other had purple. Unless the colors changed, this was not the same creature. Briefly, Athena wondered if the Isclits ran the place. How many were they?

So far, she'd only seen the cells, the hallway, and now this room. But, judging from the size of the room, the compound was rather large. She doubted this was all there was to it.

They approached the glass surrounding the forest and, just as with the wall, a door appeared out of nowhere in the side of the glass.

The next thing she knew, the devil gently pushed her forward and into the forest, just beyond the doorway.

It was sunny and Athena looked up, mildly confused. They were inside a building, weren't they? Where was the sun coming from? Unless the top of the building was open?

She filed that in the back of her mind under 'means of possible escape.'

"Try to follow their orders," the voice of the devil caught her ear and she spun to face him.

"Whose orders? And why are you telling me this?"

"You will see." He ignored her other question and turned to walk away.

"Wait." She reached her hand out towards him, then caught herself. For some reason, she didn't want him to leave. There was something about him that made her...less scared. Athena gulped as he paused.

"I'm Athena. What is your name?" This was not the place for introductions and she was sure he would just storm off and leave without answering. If someone had told her she'd be introducing herself to a man-bull-devil alien in any lifetime, she'd have given them extra pills from the dispensary because they were obviously in need of it. But here she was. Heart beating hard. Naked as the day she was born. Standing at the edge of a forest that held God knew what. And the only thing she could think of doing was to grasp at the one straw that seemed like the lesser of the evils she'd met so far.

The devil turned and looked at her, his green orbs locking with hers.

"My name," he said, "is Xul."

3

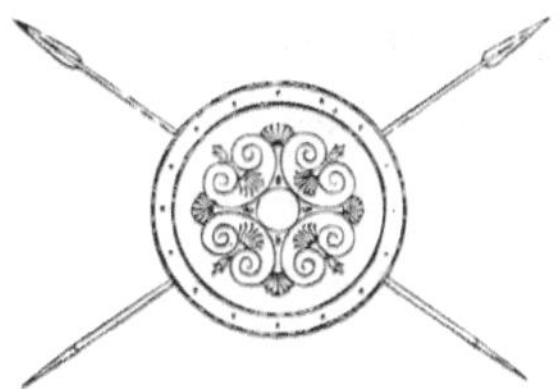

Turning around to face the forest, Athena wrapped her arms around herself.

She'd been to the Amazon once and the forest looked exactly like the one in front of her. For a moment, she wondered if that was where they were.

Was this some secret alien facility in the middle of the Amazon somewhere?

It was possible.

The Amazon was large, secluded...and dangerous.

Athena kept her ears open and her eyes sharp as she looked ahead. Only a madwoman would willingly enter a forest on her own —a forest where there could be snakes, spiders, and a host of other creatures.

Not to mention, she was naked.

The bright sun warmed the forest. There was a light breeze, but Athena couldn't see the sky. Looking outside the glass, the room was still dark.

She couldn't see the Isclit or Xul. It seemed as if she was alone.

Just then, a sound to her right caught her attention. The bushes rustled and there was an ear-splitting scream.

Athena's heart raced in her chest as the rustling approached and she glanced around for anything she could use as a weapon. The only thing she saw was a nearby rock. Grabbing it, she raised it with intent to hit whatever was approaching when a red-haired woman, naked as she was, shot out of the bushes at a mad run.

"Run!" the woman screamed as she dashed past.

Athena only had a second to think before she heard the growl of something big. She didn't need more motivation than that. Taking off after the woman, her legs pumped underneath her as she followed the woman's path. She could hardly see ahead of her with all the bushes in the way. Glimpses of the woman's red hair were the only thing telling her she was running in the right direction.

She heard the growl again and, this time, it was close.

Shit.

What the hell was it now?

Her heart felt like it was going to fall out of her chest as her lungs burned with the pressure of overexertion. When she felt like she was about to collapse, another growl made her forget all about her body about to fall apart.

She heard the woman ahead scream "Run!" again and she figured she was talking to her. Dammit, she was running; she was running as fast as she could. But in the next second, she realized the warning hadn't been meant for her as she saw another woman curled up in the leaves ahead. She was crying, with tears and what looked like mascara running down her cheeks.

"Run!" Athena screamed. She didn't know what they were running from and she didn't want to wait to find out. But the woman crying ahead just burst into fresh tears.

"Get up and run!" Athena screamed as she reached the woman, grabbing the woman's hand as she tried to pull her up. But the lady wouldn't budge.

Another growl, and this time it was really close.

"Shit! Get up!"

"I-I can't." the woman trembled. "I just want to go home." She was looking at Athena as if she wasn't really seeing her.

"Then run!" Athena screamed.

The woman looked back at her helplessly.

"Come on! Leave her, or you will be meat!" It was the red-head. She'd paused ahead and was staring at them wide-eyed, her chest heaving.

With tears in her eyes, Athena dropped the woman's hand and began running again.

She'd thought she was in hell, but this seemed even worse than hell.

At least, in hell, you knew what to expect. Hellfire, eternal damnation...and, possibly, even a devil that was green-eyed and surprisingly handsome.

But here, you didn't know what to freakin' expect.

The woman's scream was all she heard,then came the unmistakable sound of bones being crushed.

She could hardly see through her tears when an arm came out of nowhere and pulled her into the bushes. A hand covered her mouth, stifling her scream and Athena found herself looking into the redhead's sapphire eyes.

"Shh..." the red-head whispered.

Athena nodded and the woman removed her hand.

Their chests heaved as they stared at each other in silence, the sounds of the animal eating reaching their ears. The red-head motioned with her head and crept further away from the sounds of the animal eating.

Athena followed behind. The red-head obviously knew what she was doing.

"What is that?" Athena whispered when they were far enough to no longer hear the animal feasting. She couldn't think about the woman being eaten.

She couldn't.

"You wouldn't believe me if I told you," the red-head answered, motioning with her head to the right before she began moving carefully in that direction.

"Try me." If she was going to survive, she needed to know any and everything.

Knowledge was power. She might not have cared about her high-school principal drilling that in her head when she was a teen, but it sure as hell made sense right now. And she was no idiot.

She was going to soak up as much information as she could.

The red-head paused to glance back at Athena.

"A saber-toothed tiger."

"A what? Those are extin—"

"Extinct, yes. But I kid you not, I know what I saw." The red-head resumed walking and Athena stood, staring at the woman's back, trying to process what she'd just heard.

The red-head must have been mistaken.

When she realized the woman almost disappeared into the bush ahead, she picked up her pace.

Unlike Athena, whose pale skin stood out among the bushes, the red-head had daubed her body in mud, which made her less easily seen.

Smart.

As they neared a clearing, in front of them was the glass wall. Had they run in a circle? She was sure they'd been running straight ahead but, in the confusion, she wasn't sure now.

On the other side of the wall, several dozen light-blue rings hovered in the distance.

Isclits. Many of them.

Athena scowled. Glancing at the red-head, she realized she wasn't alone in her hatred for the slimy creatures.

"Fucking little shits," the red-head murmured. "First a T-Rex and now a fucking saber tooth."

"I beg your pardon?" Athena's eyes widened as she stared at the woman. "A T-Rex?"

The red-head glanced at her. "Oh, you have no idea how fucked up this place is."

Athena blinked in fast succession as her mind tried to process the rapid series of events since she'd woken up in this...place.

Where was she anyway? She still had no idea.

"Name's Diana," the red-head said, before turning her scowl back at the light-blue rings hovering in the distance.

"Athena."

"You're human?" Diana eyed her.

"Yes. You?"

Diana nodded. "You can never be sure in this place."

"What is this place?"

"That's what I've been trying to figure out for the past week."

"You've been here for a week?!"

"Yes. Maybe longer. I can't really tell."

A roar pierced Athena's ear not far from them and Athena spun in the direction of the sound, her eyes wide.

They weren't safe.

That thing that had been chasing them was on the hunt again.

"Fucking pieces of shit! Let us out!" Diana banged on the glass. "Goddammit!"

"Maybe we should run?!" Her body was teetering on that fine line between fright and flight.

A part of her wanted to run but there was that little thought that no matter how much she ran, the thing would eventually catch her anyway.

"No, it won't stop till it catches us all. We have to get those idiots' attention."

Athena turned to the wall, watching the little light-blue rings as they hovered.

The Isclits.

They had to get the Isclits' attention.

Maybe if they could break the glass.

Eyeing a large stone nearby, Athena rushed over to lift it. It was heavier than she'd thought it would be, but the heavier the better.

Using all her might, she used her body weight to hurl the stone into the glass wall.

The stone connected with the wall, causing a sound like a deep bong to echo in the vicinity as the wall seemed to absorb the impact and distribute it through a series of vibrations.

Athena stared at the area where the stone hit as another roar erupted somewhere behind her.

Shit.

It didn't break.

This wasn't just any normal glass.

She could feel her heart rate rising as she lifted her gaze to Diana, whose wild eyes were now locked with hers.

But the light-blue rings in the distance had paused moving.

They'd gotten the Isclits' attention and, at that moment, the sun seemed to dim for a second before brightening again.

"Good going," Diana breathed, her lips breaking into a smile that froze on her face. She remained like that in suspended animation and Athena was about to ask if she was alright when she realized that she couldn't move either.

Her entire body was frozen. She couldn't lift her hands; she couldn't move her legs. She couldn't even blink or move her eyes. It felt as if she was stuck in some sort of thick fluid that rendered her body motionless —as if time had stopped but her brain was still working as usual.

In the next few seconds, there was rustling in the bushes behind them. If she could move her face or mouth, she was pretty sure she'd be screaming.

Whatever had been chasing them was coming to get them...and they couldn't move! She wasn't sure if she believed it was a saber-toothed tiger but it had sounded angry and it had sounded big. That was enough for her to know she didn't want to have it over for tea.

The scream was literally stuck in her throat when the bushes moved again and she could barely make out the form of an Isclit in her peripheral vision as it emerged from the flora. She only knew it was one for sure because of the light-blue ring. That she could definitely make out. Everything else was a blur.

The only thing in focus was the last thing she was looking at before she was frozen, and that was Diana. It was eerie looking back at the redhead with her face frozen mid-smile. It was like looking at a Madame Tussaud's wax figure.

The Isclit came to hover in front of her and Athena could see that it had yellow fluorescent spots on its back but, apart from that, it looked just like the two other Isclits she'd seen so far.

Behind the Isclit was the devil himself, all green eyes and handsome bull-ness. Well, she assumed it was him. She couldn't move her gaze and her line of sight was pointing at his chest. But whoever it was had the same soft brown fuzz as he did and, in the blurry part of her peripheral vision, she could see the loincloth.

It had to be him.

But there was no more roaring. No vicious animal was bounding toward them to tear them to pieces.

Had they killed it?

She hadn't heard it die either.

"Check the. Human cargo," the Isclit spoke as it reached them in its usual broken speech.

Human cargo.

She was no flippin' cargo. Even without being able to move she could see the fire in her eyes reflected in Diana's as well.

There was a burst of air from the soldier's nostrils and Athena watched, still unable to see him fully, as he circled Diana.

"This one has no visible injuries," he said.

It was him.

She recognized the voice.

Then it was her turn to get inspected and the soldier walked over to her and circled her slowly. If her chest could heave, she would have been breathing harder.

She was naked.

Stark naked.

At least Diana had the cover of mud to hide behind. She, on the other hand, was open to the world and these aliens' scrutiny.

Xul seemed to take a little longer inspecting her, circling her slowly before he stooped in front of her so their eyes locked.

She couldn't read what was in his green gaze—his eyes were difficult to read—but they narrowed as he looked at her and his head turned to the side a little. She took that to mean he was thinking about something.

"This one has no visible injuries either," he finally said.

Suddenly, a sick feeling grew in her stomach.

Was this a game to them?

Had they put in some animal to hunt them just to see how strong they were? How long they would survive?

He did infer that she was frail.

She couldn't control the rage that spiked again. Her eyes must have been burning the fire of her anger because that same amused expression passed across his face.

She wasn't even sure how she knew that. Maybe it was how the muscles in his face relaxed as if he was laughing at a joke in his head.

The yellow dots on the Isclit pulsed.

"Species. Incompatible," it said. "Incompatibility. Removed."

The spots kept pulsing.

"Starting cargo. Eleven," the Isclit continued. "Current number. Five."

Eleven. Did it mean there were eleven humans in this place and now there were five?!

"Area. Safe," the Isclit went on. "Bidding in. Fifteen minutes."

The Isclit began hovering away on its light-blue ring and Athena glared at it for as long as it was in her line of sight.

In the next instant, the bull-man and the Isclit were both gone.

The sun seemed to dim once more and suddenly, she could move again.

It was as if the molecules that made up her body were no longer frozen in time. And, unlike when she'd been frozen, where she hadn't even realized it had happened, being given the gift of movement came with a rush. Her heart was suddenly pounding hard in her chest again, her lungs were expanding and contracting, and blood was rushing through her veins.

"What the—"

"You'll get used to it," Diana said.

"What the hell happened? I couldn't move."

"I don't know. Some sort of freeze ray. They do it so they can come in and take out whatever mistake they'd put in here with us."

"A freeze ray." She would have laughed at that just yesterday but today it wasn't so funny.

Diana nodded before turning back to face the wall. The light-blue rings were hovering outside the wall again as if nothing had just happened.

"They did it before, when they put the T-Rex in." Diana glanced at her again. "As I said, you'll get used to it."

"Oh, I'm not planning to." Athena glanced behind her, cocking her ears. She didn't hear any growls or chasing. Maybe they had removed whatever it was. "I'm not planning on staying here long enough to get used to anything."

Diana seemed to grunt at that.

"Well, maybe you won't have to. There will be bidding in fifteen minutes, it said."

"Bidding?"

"T-Rex's and saber tooths aren't the only things to worry about in this hell." Diana turned to her, a resigned look on her face. "We're about to be auctioned."

4

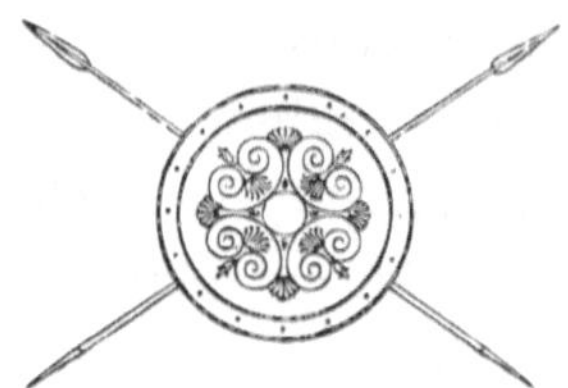

"We're about to be fucking what?"

Diana moved after dropping that bombshell, heading deeper into the brush. Athena followed behind her, batting away vines and low-hanging branches along the way.

"Auctioned to the highest bidder."

"Oh, no, no, no, no. That is not happening. We have to find a way out of here."

"We've tried." Diana stopped suddenly and Athena almost bumped into her back.

They were at another clearing that had some large boulders in the middle. By one of the boulders, it looked like three other women were huddling together using sticks to mark into the dirt on the forest floor.

"This place is like one giant rectangular box," Diana said.

"As large as a football field," a woman from the huddle piped up. Like Diana, she too had mud daubed all over her body and had even made some kind of makeshift skirt out of vines and leaves.

The woman's platinum blonde hair was a stark contrast against her muddy skin, the white strands falling down to her waist and her gray eyes stood out in her face. She was...gorgeous.

"I'm Evren," the platinum blonde stood and outstretched her hand. Her handshake was firm.

Another woman from the group stood and outstretched her hand as well. She was small, maybe just a little above five feet tall, and of Asian descent.

"I'm Song," she said, her lips shaking a little before her gaze drifted behind them to the forest. "Where's Iliana?"

"Dead," Diana said and Athena almost gasped at how matter-of-factly she'd said it. As if it was...nothing. Iliana. That must have been the woman she'd seen in the forest. The one who'd gotten eaten.

A silence enveloped the group. No one said anything and Athena's eyes darted from one woman to another. They all had that resigned look on their faces, as if it was something they'd seen happen so much, it was the new regular.

Glancing at the woman still stooping, Athena frowned slightly. She'd made no effort to stand and introduce herself like the others.

"That's Piper," Diana spoke up, stooping beside the woman as she examined the markings on the ground.

"Piper doesn't speak?" Athena asked, looking down at the silent woman's rainbow-colored hair.

"I just don't see the point in getting friendly when you might get eaten in the next five minutes," Piper mumbled, her focus still on the markings. "There's nothing here. No door. No gate. Just a frickin' glass box," she continued without pausing.

"There must be something. We're missing something," the platinum blonde, Evren, stooped beside the other two.

"Maybe we won't ever get out..." Song murmured, her gaze falling as she choked back a sob.

There was silence again.

It was a possibility no one wanted to discuss but Athena knew it was on all of their minds.

Stooping so she could look at the markings more closely, Athena glanced down at herself as she wrapped her arms across her chest.

None of the other women seemed to mind being naked. As a matter of fact, none of them were making it out to be a big deal.

Diana used a stick to point at a far corner of a rectangle they'd drawn in the ground. "This is where they put us in. The door must be there."

"Yes, but we've been there and it's just flat glass. There's no door," Piper replied.

"It must be controlled by something we can't see," Evren spoke up, her frown getting deeper.

"You mean like something we humans can't see?" Song was fiddling with her fingers and Athena noticed the dried tears on her cheeks.

Evren shrugged.

"We're somewhere in this region," Diana said, pointing to another section, far away from where the 'door' was. "And I saw the saber tooth somewhere here." She pointed to another section.

"I think that's where we first saw the T-Rex too," Piper mused.

"Wai.," Athena looked from one woman to the other. "You were really serious about the T-Rex?"

Piper's green eyes were cold. "Saber tooth. T-Rex. At this point, if they'd put us in water I'd expect to see a fucking megalodon."

"It ate one of the others..." Song came to stoop beside Athena, her shoulders shaking.

Diana threw an arm over Song's shoulder and squeezed it.

"But how? How is there a T-Rex and a saber tooth? That's impossible."

"We don't know yet. My guess is that these fuckers have been to Earth before. Picked up some shit and had it stored. And now they're back," Diana said.

"Look." Athena glanced around her at the forest. It was deathly silent. Not even wind rustled the leaves of the trees. "I'm guessing they have us enclosed in some kind of box in some forest somewhere, right? Maybe when it gets to nightfall, we can somehow get them to open that door and—"

"There's no night here," Piper cut her off.

"What?" Athena blinked, not quite comprehending.

"That," Piper raised the stick she was holding and used it to point upwards to the sky, "is no sun. It's like a giant bulb."

Athena's eyes widened as she raised her eyes to the sky.

"Whenever that shit blinks, we can't move. But at least they don't use that horrible pain remote in here," she continued. "Out there, however, they don't bother with the freeze thing. Out there, one wrong move and it's whips or the mind-numbing pain."

"I think the freeze thing has to do specifically with this habitat," Diana added.

Giant bulb. No sun. Habitat.

What the hell was this place? Really.

"I don't understand. I—" Athena took a deep breath. "A habitat?"

"My years as an ecologist tell me this is a habitat," Evren turned to her. "The temperature is perfect. They've given us a light source they know we need. They've even given us food." Evren waved her hand over to the right to a pile of fruits Athena hadn't noticed.

"And animals they think would be in the same place as us..." Diana added.

"Only those animals and us can't coexist." Piper's expression soured. "Fucking morons."

The words of the Isclit came to her head then.

"Species incompatible..." Athena whispered. "Species incompatible." She repeated, her gaze falling to the markings on the ground as everything the women were saying was slowly sinking in.

"As I said, morons," Piper snarled. "Fucking idiots. If it weren't for them, she'd still be alive."

A look at Piper and Athena saw the tears that were threatening to fall.

"Iliana?" she asked.

"Piper's sister was taken. She got..." Diana trailed off. "The T-Rex..."

Athena gulped as she stared at Piper's furious gaze. She hadn't noticed it before, but behind the angry exterior, she could see the torture and grief in the woman's eyes.

"We have to get out of here." Song rocked back and forth, pulling her knees up to her chest.

Athena gulped again. "I'm sorry, Piper."

Piper didn't respond but the stick in her hand snapped as her fingers closed around it forcefully.

Athena blinked back the tears that were suddenly forming in her eyes. She was never good when it came to comforting people but she could feel Piper's pain and anger. However, she couldn't focus on it. Focusing on it made everything feel hopeless. She'd found it was always better to change the subject. That way, she never said anything that was out of place.

"But the Isclit said there were eleven of us. From what you've said, it sounds like there were only seven. Us five and the other two that," she cleared her throat, moving her gaze away from Piper, "died."

"Isclit?" Evren raised an eyebrow.

"The slug thing. That's what it said it was called."

"Oh, we just call it Slug Thing," Evren mused. "But, to answer your question, the other four were auctioned."

Auctioned.

Yes.

Diana had mentioned that.

Suddenly, Athena's heart rate increased.

Auctioned.

"Auctioned?"

"Because of these translator things they put in our brain, we could understand what they were saying, and it sure fucking sounded like an auction." Piper wiped her eyes, still glaring as if she wasn't crying at the same time.

"Auction us to who?" Athena tried to calm her beating heart.

Just then, the sun...or rather... the giant bulb above them blinked.

"Fuck," Piper muttered, her face setting into a scowl as Song whimpered. And then, just like that, Athena found she couldn't move. Her gaze was locked on Piper's scowl and she wished she'd been looking into the forest to see what was coming towards them. She could already hear the bushes rustling.

Something moved behind her and she felt her skin prickle. Something big. Then the undeniable voice of an Isclit reached her ears.

"You will. Be moved," it said. "Failure to comply. Is pain." It circled their group and Athena noticed it had blue fluorescent spots on its back.

As the light source in the enclosure dimmed again for a second, the last of Song's whimper was released.

Piper stood slowly, her hands gripped into fists by her side.

As they all stood, Athena turned to look behind her. The large presence was still there and she half expected to see the devil looking back at her. A gasp caught in her throat as she was met face to face with the long snout of the soldier she'd passed in the corridor.

Athena jumped back in fright, and the soldier bared its jagged teeth and snarled at her.

Song whimpered again as they all huddled beside Piper, who was standing the furthest away from the thing.

An eerie laugh left the beast's mouth as it surveyed them with its yellow eyes.

"I like my dinner a little scared," it said, and Song whimpered one more time, her mouth trembling as her wide eyes fixed on the monster's teeth.

"This is not. Your food. Soldier," the Isclit said, its mouth appearing out of no visible hole on its body as usual. It sounded like a reprimand and the monster snorted. "Be quiet. Follow orders."

Athena took note of that.

The Isclits were in charge. Even over monsters like this one that looked like they could rip the Isclit apart in one bite.

"Move the. Humans to the. Viewing platform," the Isclit said, then the blue lights on its back started pulsing. "Cargo being. Moved to viewing. Platform," it said.

Diana gripped Song's shoulders to stop her from trembling.

"Humans. Follow your master," the gator-guard said as its snake-like tongue danced towards them. That spurred them to move and the monster walked behind them while the Isclit led the way in front, hovering on its light-blue ring at a reasonable pace.

Piper had been the last to move, as she'd stared fearlessly into the eyes of the yellow-eyed beast, but that meant she was at the back of the line. Athena could hear the beast licking its lips and laughing to itself. The sounds alone made shivers run down her spine. Glancing back at Piper, she saw that the woman's face was trembling with rage, her hands still balled into fists, and she prayed Piper didn't do anything to get herself killed.

Dying at the hands of that beast wouldn't be pleasant. Not that dying was pleasant. But there were so many other better ways to go than to be eaten alive.

Her mild distraction caused her not to see how the Isclit opened the door to the glass wall, as they were now moving out of the enclosure and heading into the dim area outside. She hoped to God that one of the other women had taken the time to notice.

The Isclit led them to a raised platform and ordered them not to move as the yellow-eyed monster took its place behind them.

Song was still trembling, with Evren trying to comfort her, while Diana was busy trying to peer into the darkness that faced them.

In the next moment, the entire area was filled with light.

The sudden brightness made Athena shade her eyes as she squinted, her eyes adjusting to the glare.

What she saw next made her eyes go wide.

5

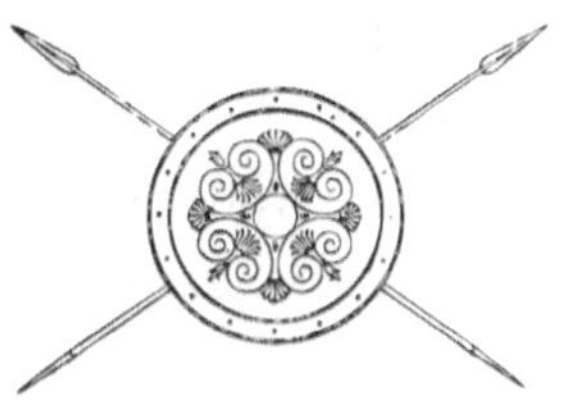

In front of them were rows and rows of...aliens.

And not Isclits or devils or stone men or weird gator-guards. It was other weird green things with big dark eyes and puffed up necks. They were all dressed in what looked like white robes crested with gold.

They looked like...toads? It was the closest animal Athena could think of to compare them to, except they were way too big to be toads. They were all different in size and all varying shades of green.

"Let the. Auction begin," the Isclit announced and a loud murmur went through the alien crowd.

Song whimpered, tears running down her face now and Evren glanced at Athena, gripping her hand and squeezing it softly.

They were all they had. On Earth, they'd been complete strangers but now, they were like sisters.

It was the five of them against what looked to be at least a hundred aliens.

And they were about to be auctioned for God knows what.

The green toad-like aliens were pointing at them and emitting loud grunts, some obviously getting excited as they grunted quickly, moving their large bodies in their seats in what looked like excited jumping.

"Let's get that one," one of them murmured to another sitting beside it. It outstretched its arm to point at Song and Song shuddered, unable to control the new wave of tears that ran down her cheeks.

Athena's gaze fell on the outstretched arm and gulped. It was bony and covered with what looked like fluid-filled bubbles. It looked like a pus-filled, diseased, two-fingered arm.

Totally vomit-inducing material.

"No," the other one said, "she would be too easy for our Ceqtaq to decimate." It moved its huge dark gaze over their group till its gaze fell on Piper.

"Oh," the first one cooed, and Athena realized, judging from its smaller body and the fact that its face was a little softer (if you could call it that), it must be the female in the relationship. "But I would love to see the Ceqtaq play with this little...frail toy." The female made a sound like bubbles popping and Athena assumed it was laughing.

She was sure Song could hear every word they were saying. A glance at Song showed the woman's entire small frame was trembling.

"No," the male said. "I like a fight." He pointed at Piper. "We'll get this one. It looks...angry." He emitted a bubbly sound, deeper than its partners, and Athena assumed it was laughing as well.

Piper snarled at them.

Fearless, she was, and Athena's strength renewed from Piper's anger. She wasn't going down without a fight either.

Athena turned back to the crowd of aliens, her gaze resolute, when a spotlight was shone over her. Evren squeezed her hand again.

"Looks like you're first," Evren murmured. "Good luck."

Wait, what?

Athena's heart beat hard in her chest as she gripped Evren's fingers as if it was the last thing connecting her to Earth.

She wasn't ready to be auctioned.

She hadn't had enough time to gather information about the place.

She wasn't ready.

"Our human. Cargo." The Isclit with the blue spots spoke, its voice booming in the entire room and Athena took the moment to look around, realizing that with all the things happening, she hadn't had the chance to look around till then.

They had definitely not been outside when they'd been behind the glass walls. Looking at it now, it looked like the glass enclosure rose into the sky, well, what she'd thought was the sky, but on this side, it told her they were definitely still in a building...or ship, wherever they were.

The glass enclosure only presented the illusion that they were not totally enclosed.

"Bidding for. This one. Starts now," the Isclit's voice boomed again and Athena wondered how it was managing to get its voice to project so loudly.

But she didn't have time to think about that because, in the next instant, her body was being lifted into the air as the spotlight hovered over her.

Trying hard to clutch on to Evren's hand proved futile as she was lifted over the other women's heads and slowly spun around.

To her horror, she saw little blue cards lighting up as the aliens began bidding. But she couldn't scream. She couldn't actually move.

It seemed as if the light had the same effect as the one within the enclosure. She was being spun around, naked for all of them to see, and there was nothing she could do about it.

She could still hear Song's whimpers but that was soon drowned out as the murmurs of the aliens reached her ears.

Blue card after blue card was raised, each with different markings she couldn't understand. She assumed those were numbers or amounts of currency as, the more the markings seemed to increase on the cards, the more excited the crowd became.

A loud bubbly sound echoed through the room and Athena could see that whichever alien was emitting the sound was holding a golden card.

She guessed that was the alien that won.

She was sold.

Sold to a pus-filled toad.

As she was lowered back to the platform, her eyes met the wide eyes of the other women. Their gazes all communicated the same thing.

They were all scared.

No matter how angry or determined they all were, none of them knew what happened after they left that room and the possibilities were endless.

Her feet barely touched the platform before the yellow-eyed monster who'd been standing guard behind them approached.

He was swift, his arm stretching to close his hand around her neck in one movement.

Athena struggled against him, grabbing onto the arm as it lifted her into the air. Her scream only caused a series of bubble-like sounds to erupt in the room.

They were laughing at this.

They thought it was funny.

The guard snarled at her, sticking out its forked tongue to hover just in front of her face and no matter how she kicked and squirmed, she couldn't free herself.

His grip was too tight. He was too strong.

The thought that this was the reason he'd been standing there all along crossed her mind.

He was just there to swallow her whole.

This auction wasn't an auction in the sense that she'd thought. It was just an exotic feeding frenzy—with her being the exotic meal up for tasting.

But as the thoughts crossed her mind, the yellow-eyed beast unhooked a chain from its waist and fastened it around her neck, releasing her immediately so she fell back onto the platform.

The pain from the fall shot up through the arm that she'd landed on and she was vaguely aware that Evren was helping her up.

"Move!" the yellow-eyed monster ordered, yanking on the chain as he pulled her toward the alien holding the golden card.

The chain dug into her neck and she was sure the metal was cutting into her skin.

She was restrained.

It was frickin' painful and Athena held onto the chain, trying to slip her fingers between the metal and her skin so she could create some space and get some relief.

Was this what the devil, Xul, had been meant to do to her from the start?

Thank God he hadn't.

The thought of him made her glance around the room but she didn't see him. It didn't matter though. He was an alien like the rest of them. What help would he be now?

As they approached the alien with the golden card, Athena wished time would slow.

Not knowing what was about to happen next was terrifying and she already missed the familiarity of having other humans around her.

Walking away from them was like going into the unknown. An unknown that was filled with otherworldly species that were treating her like cattle.

When they reached the alien with the golden card, its huge eyes roved over Athena's body and she watched in horror as its thick, heavy tongue ran over its lips. Judging from that, it was thinking one of two things.

Either it wanted to eat her...or it wanted to...

Athena shuddered at the thought, pushing it away from her mind. It wouldn't come to that.

She'd rather die than have this disgusting creature inside her.

Trying to hide the fear behind her eyes, she glared at the alien as the yellow-eyed monster placed the chains in the thing's hand.

The thing held the chains as it eyed her, still licking its lips.

They were even more hideous up close and this one was huge, its puffed up neck hanging over its robe.

"I am your new master," it said, and Athena gritted her teeth. The fact that she could understand what it said thanks to the translator thing didn't help the fact that it was terrifying-looking. Speaking English didn't make it less strange. If anything, being able to understand it made everything worse. It was an intelligent being. One that could communicate. And it was its intelligence that scared her.

If she'd been on an alien ship with less intelligent life-forms, her chances of survival would have probably tripled. Now, she wasn't sure what chances of survival she had.

Everything was just so strange. So different.

The voice of the Isclit who was running the auction boomed again. "Next up, is this specimen."

Athena glanced back towards the women to see Piper being lifted into the air in the beam of light.

"Wait!" The alien beside her pronounced, rising slowly on legs Athena could not see as they were hidden underneath its long robes. "I need a guard to transport me to my ship," it continued. "Me and my newly acquired pet." It licked its lips again as its eyes fell on Athena and she visibly cringed under its gaze.

The Isclit paused, its eyes turning to look over at their location.

"We do not. Provide guards," the Isclit said.

"Are you denying the request of a High Tasqal?" Any murmurs in the room were now hushed, the only sound Athena could hear was Song's soft whimpers.

Another Isclit hovered over toward them, its purple fluorescent spots glowing in the light and Athena wondered if it was the same Isclit she had seen when she'd just woken up.

"We always. Respect the wishes. Of the High Tasqals," the Isclit with the purple spots said, its mouth appearing from nowhere.

She would never get used to that.

"We will send. A guard to. Your quarters, sire." The Isclit bowed its eyes and Athena frowned as she watched it do so. It didn't have a head, so she supposed that was its way of showing respect?

The High Tasqal grunted and yanked on her chain, causing Athena to inhale sharply as she was jerked forward.

"Come," it said and licked its lips again as it began to leave the room.

Turning her gaze to the women she'd left on the platform, Piper was still suspended motionless in the air while the others had their wide eyes on her.

Neither said anything but it was in all their gazes.

They wished her luck.

6

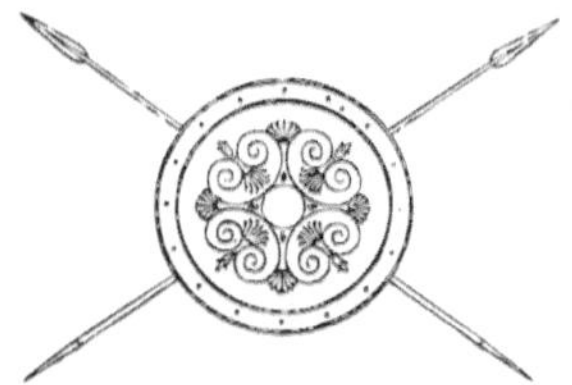

The High Tasqal moved slowly out of the room and Athena kept her gaze on the other women till they turned a corner and she could no longer see them.

Turning to look at the back of the High Tasqal as it walked in front of her, Athena weighed her options.

It was just the two of them.

If she managed to get break free, maybe she could somehow get away. It didn't look armed but the fact that she wasn't being escorted by a guard worried her.

Was the High Tasqal more dangerous than it looked?

From what she could see, she could probably outrun it.

Probably.

Bile rose in her throat as her gaze fell to its bubble-filled arm. It was beyond disgusting.

"Where are you taking me?" she ventured. Maybe it would talk to her.

"Silence," the thing said.

Well, speaking was off the table. She wasn't going to give it any reason to harm her. The chain around her neck was enough pain at the moment and if this thing was anything like the Isclits, it could have a remote hiding somewhere within its body ready to make her writhe in agony.

Maybe that was why there were no guards escorting them.

Judging from its robes and the fact it had called itself a "High" Tasqal, she figured it must be in the upper echelons of its society. That made the fact that there was no escort even more curious.

A High Tasqal.

Athena's eyes bore into the thing's back as it pulled her along.

What the hell did a "Low" Tasqal look like, because this thing looked like it belonged in the sewers, away from society.

The High Tasqal paused in front of a wall and a door materialized in front of them, opening to a room that was dimly lit in a purple hue. The thing's broad frame had been blocking her but as far as she could see, it had done nothing to open the door.

With a grunt, it pulled her into the room and Athena's eyes adjusted to the purple light.

For some reason, she'd been expecting another room like the cell she'd been in but this room was completely different.

In the center was what looked like a mini waterfall that cascaded into a pool. Except whatever was running down the rocks wasn't water. It was a thick purple fluid.

There was something else too. An odor of some kind. She wasn't quite sure what the smell was. Athena tried to ignore it by focusing across the room, where there was a large slab....only it wasn't a hard flat rock. She could see, even without touching it, that it was made of some sort of billowy material. Judging from the size of it she assumed it could only be one thing.

A bed.

Directly across from it was another slab. The only thing was that this one looked as if it had someone chained to it.

Another human. Another woman she hadn't seen before.

The woman raised her head as they entered the room and their eyes met. There was no denying what was there.

Pure terror.

She was trembling so hard, the chains were clanging against the slab, and Athena noticed something else.

There were what looked like small bubble-filled sores appearing all over the woman's body. Sores that looked quite similar to the ones on the High Tasqal.

With a grunt, the High Tasqal pulled Athena across the room before it suddenly stopped walking and turned to face her. She could hear the bubbles in its throat as it laughed to itself.

"My human," it murmured, its wide mouth hardly moving. "Your species is frail but highly fertile. You will do well to be my slave."

Taking a few steps away from it, Athena found her back was against a wall. The High Tasqal advanced slowly, the laughter still bubbling in its throat.

"My pet," it murmured.

Stretching out its bubble-filled hand, it unhooked the chain from her neck and Athena rubbed the area, watching the High Tasqal warily, her gaze darting from it to the woman who was still trembling on the slab.

She'd thought she'd be alone with it but it seemed the woman was one of the others who had been auctioned before Athena arrived.

The High Tasqal reached out again and grabbed her before she could duck out of the way.

Despite that its hands were so much thinner than its body, it was remarkably strong.

It lifted her in the air, its hand locking around her neck, as it turned its head slowly from side to side inspecting her.

"It is the first time the Isclits have returned to your planet in many years," it murmured, ignoring the fact that she was struggling in its grasp.

"I am pleased with their find this time. A simple sample of what can be farmed." It used its other hand to pull at her arms and legs.

"Intelligent life on such an undeveloped rock," it continued murmuring. "Just the right size for breeding." Its gaze dropped to her privates and a chill ran through Athena's entire frame.

"Or for our sexual entertainment." Another series of bubbles popping erupted from the High Tasqal. "The Tasqals will be happy with this find."

Athena said nothing. The Tasqal's words were too jarring. Too revealing. It was painting her future right in front of her and it was a life she definitely did not want to live.

"I will give you two options, human," it said. "As I have two." It glanced back at the woman on the slab and another series of bubble sounds erupted in its throat.

"Choose to be my sex pet, here for my sexual pleasure and I will not breed you." It looked back at her. "Or choose to be my mate and bear my spawn."

Athena gritted her teeth.

Two unbelievably generous options those were.

As she struggled against the hand holding her up, her gaze fell once again to the woman on the slab.

"It doesn't matter!" the woman screamed. "It will rape you anyway. It is only playing games!"

"Silence!" The High Tasqal spun so fast, it made Athena dizzy.

She could see tears running down the woman's face but the woman said nothing more.

Turning back its attention on her, the High Tasqal's mouth opened and Athena watched its heavy tongue emerge, dripping with saliva. Kicking and struggling against the arm that was holding her up did nothing to help her situation.

If anything, her efforts to have him release her were spurring the High Tasqal on.

It was just about to lick her when it paused.

"You Earth scent is distracting," it said, slipping its tongue back into its mouth and releasing her. She fell to the floor.

"You must prepare yourself," the High Tasqal said, turning away, and Athena realized she'd been holding her breath. "Prepare yourself with spices." It gestured over to a side of the room with what looked like another high waterfall, except this one looked like it actually had water running from it.

Was it asking her to take a bath?

Athena frowned, her breathing hard and shallow.

The High Tasqal had said enough for her to understand exactly what her purpose was. And what was worse, this was just the beginning.

She was a sample.

She assumed the other human women and men she'd seen were samples too.

Samples for a greater purpose.

Earth was in danger. Even if she did escape, it would mean only delaying the inevitable.

The realization had her frozen on the floor. Everybody she knew, everybody she loved, they were all in danger.

The High Tasqal grunted and turned its head toward where the door was supposed to be, as if sensing something. Its voice boomed as it commanded, "Enter."

The door materialized out of the wall and Athena realized the doorway was filled with something big. The light shining behind the guest made it hard for her to see the face but the horns protruding from his head gave her a good idea of who it was.

Xul entered the room and his green eyes found her immediately. He scanned her body quickly before glancing at the High Tasqal, then at the other woman on the slab.

She was sure she saw the bone in his jaw tick.

"Sire," he said, addressing the High Tasqal before moving to stand by the door.

The High Tasqal grunted and moved over to the purple waterfall in the middle of the room.

Athena choked back a gasp as the robes fell from its body to the floor.

Its entire body was filled with the bubble-like sores and it looked like one massive dark green, leathery pouch standing on two flat legs. Lifting its body, it stepped over into the waterfall and settled itself in the thick purple fluid.

Athena tried not to gag.

Damn, it was hideous.

Were there no beautiful aliens?

Her gaze fell on Xul at that thought and she glanced away quickly, realizing his green eyes were still focused on her.

"Prepare yourself," the High Tasqal said, again motioning to the tall waterfall in the corner. "With spices."

Prepare herself for what?

So it could use her for its sexual pleasure?

No, thank you.

When it noticed that she hadn't moved, it turned its head to look at her.

"Hmm," it murmured, reaching its bony hand to the side to grab something off the rocks. Athena's eyes widened and her heartbeat sped up as she realized what it was.

The torture remote. So it did have one.

A bubbly sound began in the High Tasqal's throat as it watched her response.

"Prepare yourself," it said more firmly than before.

Athena took a few seconds to run through options in her mind. Her eyes darted around the room, looking for anything she could use for defense. But the only weapon in the room was the spear being held by the devil and she was sure she couldn't wrestle it from him.

She could probably outrun the High Tasqal, judging from how its body looked, but she knew she wouldn't get far with the devil in the way. Plus, she'd have to find a way to release the other woman so they could escape together.

She also still hadn't figured out how the doors opened and closed. Even if she did, she still had no idea of the layout of the place and it seemed to be teeming with aliens anyway.

Damn. She needed a light at the end of this tunnel, and soon. She needed to warn the other women. They needed to hatch an escape plan. And, somehow, they needed to save Earth from a potential invasion.

She must have taken too long in her thoughts because, in the next instant, a pain like no other coursed through her veins, causing her to collapse to the floor on her hands and knees. It felt like burning and ice in her veins at the same time, and Athena gasped for air but found she couldn't even breathe, as the pain had knocked the wind out of her.

It lasted only for a few seconds as the High Tasqal released the button on the remote but it left her collapsed on the floor writhing as the last of the pain left her body.

Thick, warm liquid ran down her lips and she realized her nose was bleeding.

Athena looked up at the High Tasqal, its expression unreadable, and was thankful it hadn't decided to punish her further.

Getting to her shaky feet, she stood and wiped the remainder of blood running from her nose.

"Prepare yourself," the High Tasqal repeated and Athena swallowed hard, glancing at the remote in its hand.

It had felt as if her body was being ripped in two. Whatever they'd done to her while she'd been unconscious, it was controlled by that remote.

If she had any chances of getting away, she needed to get rid of that remote first.

Glancing over at the devil standing by where the door should be, Athena gulped again.

Another sound erupted from the High Tasqal and it ordered, its voice commanding, "Make it prepare itself, with spices." It motioned to the devil, and a snort of hot air escaped the devil's nostrils as he moved forward, his spear glinting in the light.

"I do not wish to damage the sample, as I must be able to use it for pleasure tonight," the High Tasqal continued, rising from the purple liquid as it moved toward the other woman on the slab.

The woman's eyes widened as she started clanging on the chains and Athena stared in horror.

Taking her by the arm, Xul pulled her over to the waterfall and placed her underneath it.

A scream from behind them made her try to spin and look but Xul was blocking her view. Holding firm on her shoulders, he kept her facing the waterfall.

"You do not want to see," he murmured, his voice so low she was sure the High Tasqal could not hear him.

Another scream erupted behind them and a deep moan from the High Tasqal reached her ears.

Twisting out of his grasp, Athena spun so she could see what was happening and the world paused for a second as reality seemed to shatter right before her very eyes.

The High Tasqal was on top of the woman, its sex organ deep within her, as it thrusted into the woman over and over again.

The horror in front of her made her spring into action immediately, as Athena made to dash towards them. She didn't know what she'd do but she needed to do something.

But two strong arms circled her and pulled her back under the waterfall.

"Do not risk yourself," Xul spoke low and level but she could see he was speaking through clenched teeth. "She is already infected. We cannot save her."

His words puzzled her and she raised her fiery gaze to his.

"It is raping her! I have to do something!" she replied. Trying to keep her voice low was hard but the screams of the woman echoing through the chamber was good cover for their conversation.

Xul studied her for a second and she was sure she could see pain in his eyes.

But why? Wasn't he a part of the same team?

"She is already dead," he said. "Do not interfere or the same may happen to you."

A low roar echoed in the chamber next and both she and Xul turned to the scene to see that the woman was biting down hard on the High Tasqal's neck.

Raising itself above her, pure fury emanated from the Tasqal's being.

"You dare try to harm me, you pathetic worm?!" it bellowed.

And with one movement, it took the woman's head between its hands and twisted her neck.

A scream left Athena's throat as the woman's body suddenly went limp.

It'd killed her. Just like that. As if she was nothing.

Terrified, her heart hammered in her chest as the High Tasqal turned to look at her.

"Puny humans," it said, pausing as it regarded her. "I guess you will have to be both my mate and my entertainment."

Athena shuddered as she backed away into Xul's hard body.

She was sure she felt him stiffen at the words.

"Bring her," the High Tasqal said.

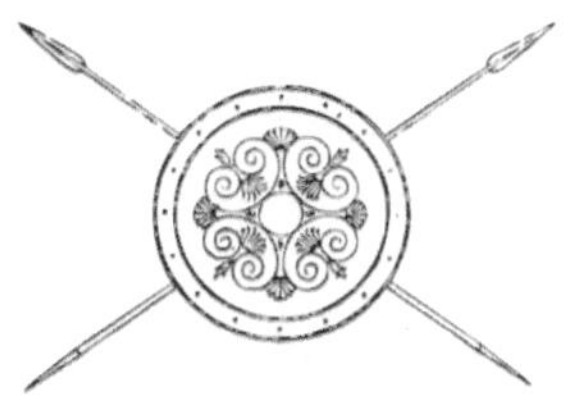

As Xul pulled her back into the center of the room, Athena found that she was trembling.

She needed to do something. Anything.

It seemed that either way she took it, she was going to die anyway.

"Good," the High Tasqal's voice boomed as it regarded her and the sounds of bubbles popping came next as it laughed.

But despite that it had just killed the woman, it appeared to have pleased itself because it was now slipping into its robes once again.

"Guard, you will transport us to my ship," the High Tasqal hardly glanced at Xul as it spoke. Grabbing the chains she'd been wearing earlier, it approached her and all she could see was its hands circling the woman's head as it twisted her neck.

A dry heave threatened to come forth as she glanced behind it at the woman's limp body.

Backing away from the High Tasqal, her hands gripped into the billowy material of the bed. It was like cotton wool and her fingers sunk into it.

The High Tasqal approached and gripped her neck with the same hands it had just used to kill another and Athena swallowed hard, fighting back the slew of emotions rising in her stomach.

As it secured the chain around her neck, it led her toward the door, pulling her so hard that the chain bit into her neck and a large piece of the wool-like material ripped off the bed.

She was about to let it fall when the thought came to her that she might be able to use it later.

Anything might be useful at this point.

Trying to ignore the pain around her neck, she tried not to look at the woman's body as she was pulled past it.

She was already close to tears at the vicious act. She couldn't look.

Wrapping the wool-like material around her waist, they were in the hallway when she tied another piece of the material around her breasts.

Walking down the corridor, the bright light had a disinfecting effect on the surroundings. But she knew better.

There was blood behind these walls.

Xul was in front, the muscles in his hard back rippling as he walked.

He was different from the others. Very different.

More...caring?

Moving her gaze from him to the High Tasqal, it was a bit strange that two species that were so different could exist in the same galaxy.

Now that was a thought.

What if she was no longer in the Milky Way?

She still had no idea if she was in a building or a ship. It looked like it was a building, like some kind of alien base, but judging from the size of it, she could be mistaken.

But if it was a building, was it disguised on Earth somewhere?

And, if it was a starship, was it anywhere near Earth?

They came to stand in front of a wall and soon a door appeared and opened to what looked like a lift. Stepping in first, Xul stood to the back before the High Tasqal entered next, pulling her in to stand beside it.

The door closed and the lift descended.

"We will take a transport ship from the dock," the High Tasqal spoke. "You will pilot me to my ship."

She assumed it was speaking to Xul.

One look at Xul showed that he was wearing that same unreadable expression. But his eyes were hard and his jaw was set.

His words back in the room repeated in her mind.

Once again, he had tried to protect her.

But why?

In the next few seconds, the elevator stopped moving and the doors opened to a large bay.

Unlike what she had seen before, this section of the place was filled with large metal pipes that networked overhead.

In front of them, several small starships were parked and there were Isclits and yellow-eyed monster guards everywhere.

Not only that, there were other aliens in chains just like her. Some were being dragged mercilessly and being loaded into the small ships. Others were being pushed into a corner where she assumed they were to stand and wait.

From what she could see, there were no other humans there and she wondered whether that was a good or a bad thing.

As the High Tasqal pulled on the chain, leading her through the commotion, something moving along a conveyor belt caught Athena's attention.

It was large and hairy, like a lion, but the two long teeth protruding down either side of his jaw had Athena's mouth falling open in shock.

It was the saber tooth.

The other women hadn't been lying. That meant the T-Rex... Athena's eyes darted around the area quickly. If it was there, she was sure it wouldn't be hard for her to miss.

The High Tasqal pulled hard on the chain again and Athena winced, only just realizing that they'd come to stand in front of an empty starship.

Looking the thing over, it looked like something you would see at an amusement park as one of the rides.

Glancing at Xul, she watched him open the starship. The door opened like that of a DeLorean and reminded her of Back to the Future.

Then the High Tasqal entered, taking the seat beside where the captain should be.

"Get in," Xul said, his voice gruff.

Athena shot him a look and then climbed into the back of the starship, jumping as Xul slammed the doors closed before entering the captain's seat.

"Make it swift," the High Tasqal said and Xul grunted in response.

The engine started in the next instant and the starship hummed peacefully. Athena watched the two aliens in front of her secure their seat belts and looked around if there was one for her. Finding the belt, she secured herself to the back seat and tried to calm her beating heart.

She had no idea what to expect next and it terrified her.

This was another unknown she was heading into.

Xul began pushing buttons and the ship slowly lifted into the air. Athena's eyes widened as she looked out the window. As the ship rose, the Isclits and other aliens who were busy in the cargo hold got smaller and smaller. They were going high and she thanked the heavens she was not afraid of heights.

In the next few seconds, the ship moved forward into another area, where there was nothing but a wide-open space. Behind, she could see the doors closing on the cargo hold.

This must be an airlock, she thought. She had watched enough sci-fi movies to figure that out.

In front, two large doors the size of giants began opening and Athena gasped audibly.

It was space. Frickin' space. She almost forgot who she was in the midst of as she leaned forward, her eyes widening.

It wasn't how she'd imagined it.

In her head, space was full of stars but all she could see outside was a black void.

"Exit in three...two...one," Xul grunted and then the ship shot forward with a sudden burst of speed.

Athena's eyes widened further as she looked outside the window.

Behind them, from where they'd just left, was a gargantuan spaceship. It dwarfed the little spaceship they were traveling in a thousand times over.

So that was where she'd been all that time? Not some building in the Amazon. Not on Earth at all.

As the ship moved forward, Athena kept searching for anything she could see that was even vaguely familiar. Earth, the moon, Mars? But there was nothing. The only other thing that was close to them was another ship that was not far in front. It was smaller than the huge one on which she'd just been and she assumed that's where they were headed.

They were moving fast. Behind them, the large ship was slowly getting farther and farther away.

"You are heading in the wrong direction, guard," the High Tasqal's voice boomed in the small spaceship.

"It appears the coordinates are not working, sire," Xul answered.

"Then make them work lest we go off course," the High Tasqal ordered.

The exchange caused Athena to pull her eyes away from the window.

Yes, the High Tasqal was right. They were no longer heading straight toward what she assumed was the High Tasqal's ship. Instead, they were heading off at an angle into deeper space.

The starship began to shake and Athena gripped onto the seatbelt.

This wasn't good.

"It also appears the engine is failing," Xul said, his voice lacking much emotion.

As the ship shuddered, a series of beeps and warning lights began flashing. Athena gripped tighter to her seat. What exactly happened when a ship fell out of space?

"Ulruq, of the Tasqal Legion," Xul suddenly said and the High Tasqal visibly stiffened.

"You dare call me by my name?!"

Xul ignored the Tasqal and continued, "Your race will pay for its crimes."

Reaching behind his neck and under his hair, Xul pulled forth something that glistened in the light.

It was a dagger with a long curved blade.

In one swift movement that neither she nor the High Tasqal expected, Xul placed the dagger at the High Tasqal's throat.

The High Tasqal's eyes widened before its gaze settled as if it was thinking about its next move.

But Xul didn't give it time to think.

"This," he said, "is for Xan."

The blade went deep and the High Tasqal only had a moment to try to lurch toward Xul before its eyes suddenly went still and it fell back in its seat.

Athena stifled a scream.

Just what the actual hell?!

But when it wasn't one thing, it seemed to be something else.

Another jerk of the ship caused Xul to hold on to the wheel to try and steer the thing but now they were falling hard and they were falling fast.

In front of them, she could see what looked like a brown planet coming into view quickly.

Too quickly.

They were going to crash and there was nothing that was going to stop that.

8

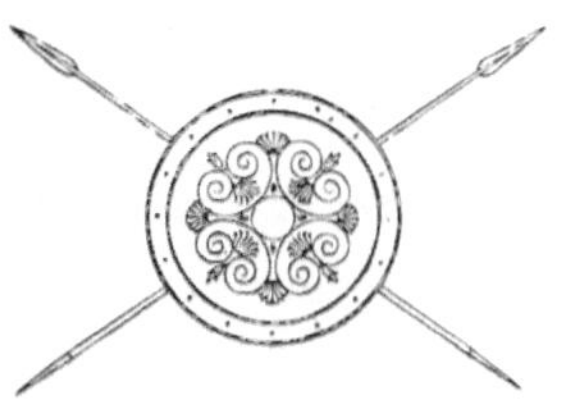

Xul's eyes shot open. His vision was slightly blurred, but they'd made it.

After the danger of entering the atmosphere, he'd tried his best to land the ship as delicately as he could.

It had crashed nose-first into the ground below.

Ah well. He'd tried.

Glancing at the body of Ulruq, the High Tasqal, Xul snarled. The Tasqal looked even uglier in death than it did in life. Their souls were the dirtiest of all.

Its thick blood was running down its robe. Knowing the Tasqal's nature, he'd made sure to slice the thing's neck so the blood wouldn't squirt forward and cover him.

Heaving himself from his seat, he was happy to see that he had no injuries. The front of the ship was mangled though, but it seemed it had borne the brunt of the damage.

Judging from the narrow stream of light entering from overhead, it also seemed as if the ship had been almost split in two.

A kick to the door didn't produce an exit. It seemed the Isclit's had wired everything to a central system and because that central system was out, the doors were sealed shut.

It was nonsensical technology.

What was one to do then in situations like this?

Glancing at his sokja, he eyed the hole again. He could use it to make the narrow hole bigger to provide a way to leave the ship.

Yes, that was what he would have to do.

Positioning himself in the small space between the front and back seats, his eyes roved over the female. She'd told him her name once, but he didn't recall it. He had taken to think of her as the golden-haired human instead.

She had struck him as different from the first time he'd walked into the holding cell. Something about her defiance in the face of the odds against her had been entertaining.

He had never seen another being so oblivious to their lack of power. Even teens from his home planet had more strength than humans—both human males and females.

It made him wonder what their young were like. If it was any indication, the thing was born weak and strongly dependent.

She'd taken the time to cover herself with material that would only last for a few days. Xul huffed out some air through his nose. It was ingenious, he had to admit. But the material was not going to stand up to the trek that they had ahead of them.

She would realize that soon enough.

That is, *if* she decided to come with him.

If it was his choice, she would still be on the ship, not here compromising his mission.

He could already tell that she was going to slow him down.

Peering at her more closely, his gaze ran down her body.

Apart from her golden hair, her face was bland with no distinct markings. Where he was from, the women had horns just like the males, though smaller. But it seemed that humans had no such thing. Despite that, he had to admit that her face was...delicate. Soft, like the petals of a flower, almost.

From what he'd seen, she had no tail. Peculiar.

Apart from those things, she was very similar to the women of his people and he imagined that Earth was a bit like his planet for such a species to develop there.

She looked so...delicate.

Xul closed his eyes and shook his head.

He had not fostered such thoughts about a woman in a long time. Preventing the rise of the Tasqals had been his sole focus for years.

She was lying limply and a deep gash was in her forehead, probably from a piece of flying shrapnel.

He hadn't meant to scare her but the situation could not have been prevented. Even now, her screams rang in his ears.

It was unfortunate that she was caught in such a predicament. It was just a case of being in the wrong place at the wrong time. After all, he had not anticipated her presence.

Moving closer, he peered at her. He could tell that she was breathing but her lungs were obviously small, judging from her body size.

That meant the journey was going to be extra hard for both of them. Hard on her because her body was going to be put to the ultimate test, and hard on him because he was sure she had no idea what was in store for her.

A glance outside the ship told him a sandstorm was brewing.

That meant they needed to get moving, and fast.

The Isclits would send a probe to search for any survivors but he knew they wouldn't venture into the desert.

It was far too dangerous.

Glancing back at the female, a frown creased his brow.

He needed to focus on his mission and she was already proving to be a distraction.

An unexpected, fiery, golden-haired one.

9

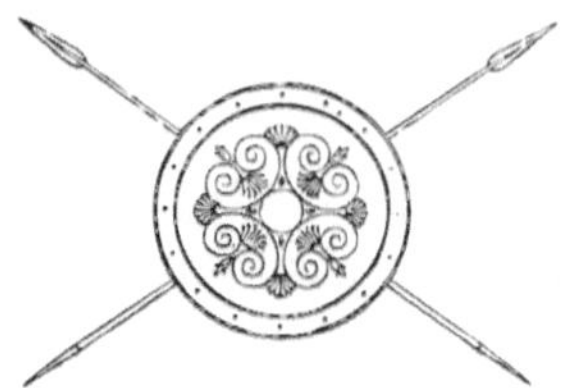

Everything hurt.

Everything.

Athena groaned as she managed to open her eyes a little.

Flashing images of the last few minutes came back to her mind.

Hurtling through space. Entering the planet's atmosphere.

Feeling as if she was going to burn up as they fell from the sky, her own screams echoed in her ears.

The next thing was the pain in her head.

Now, as her eyes fluttered open and her vision focused, the face peering down at her made her jump backward, causing a sharp pain to shoot up through her neck.

Xul was frowning down at her and he was close, way too close. Despite the pain in her head and neck, her senses still picked up his earthy smell.

"What are you doing?" Athena squeezed her eyes shut for a second. Her head was really throbbing. This whole thing reminded her of when she'd just woken up in that cell to see him and had thought he was the devil.

She would never get used to his horns and it made her wonder what else was different about him.

Xul frowned, his large hand coming toward her.

Despite the pain, Athena scrambled back but the seat belt she'd so dutifully fastened around herself was now holding her put. It might have saved her life a few seconds ago—God knows she wouldn't have wanted to hurtle through the front of the ship as it fell through the sky—but now it was holding her hostage.

Shit. He'd just murdered someone—no, something—in cold blood right in front of her eyes. She couldn't imagine what he was planning on doing to her.

He must have seen the fear in her eyes because his hand paused just over her head.

"I will not harm you," he said.

Athena gulped, the fear still making her heart beat hard.

A glance behind him made her eyes widen even more.

It was utter carnage. The front of the ship was crushed in like when you crumple an empty Coke can.

Above her, the top of the ship was split open.

A few more glances told her they were in a vast expanse of what looked like sand. Sand as far as her eyes could see and, in the distance, were what looked like two suns.

If she didn't know any better, she'd have thought they'd landed on the planet Tatooine from Star Wars.

As long as the Hutt gangsters weren't around...she had enough problems on her hands.

Although, funny enough, the High Tasqal could give Jabba the Hutt a run for his money.

But the High Tasqal was dead and she wasn't sure if she would live either. Not with a murderer right in front of her.

"Oh my God," Athena breathed, her gaze wandering to the seat in front where the body of the High Tasqal lay limply.

"You call on spirits but they will not hear you. Not here," Xul said as he turned and grabbed his spear. "This is a land of nothing. Not even the spirits dwell here."

Athena scuttled back some more, her eyes on his spear.

There was a myriad of thoughts in her head and none of them were good.

In one deft movement, Xul lodged his spear in the roof of the ship and sliced it open further.

That only made her feel faint. Was he really that strong or had they been flying in essentially a toy ship? If it was the latter, she was lucky they hadn't burned up when they'd entered the atmosphere.

"My sokja is made from a rare metal from my home planet," Xul said, answering the question in her eyes. "It can cut through the Isclit's substandard architecture."

Athena nodded. Uh-huh. As long as he kept it pointing away from her then, that would be fine.

After a glance back at the High Tasqal, she watched Xul warily as she unbuckled the seat belt. Her head was still throbbing but she would just have to bear the pain.

As she moved slowly towards the door of the ship, she kept her eyes on the large alien busy working on opening the ship's roof.

"The doors no longer open," he said, glancing down at her, slight amusement on his face again.

"What made you think I was heading toward the door?"

Xul didn't answer but, instead, went back to widening the gap in the roof.

"Your species is strange," he said.

"My species is *human*." Athena frowned. "And, for the second time, I am *not* strange. What's strange is being taken from your lovely monotonous life to be thrown into some sci-fi fantasy that isn't really a fantasy because all I've been experiencing so far is terror."

She didn't know why she was talking to him.

Why was she talking to him?

Xul glanced down at her again before continuing what he was doing.

Before long, he'd made a large gap in the roof.

"Come," he said.

Athena looked up at him, unmoving. He didn't expect her to just dash into his arms, did he?

A look of slight frustration crossed over his features.

"You can stay stuck inside the ship with the High Tasqal, then. It will start rotting as soon as the double suns fully rise. Its body is not made for survival in this atmosphere."

Athena screwed up her nose.

So it was either stay with an alien or leave with an alien.

So many choices.

Begrudgingly sitting more upright, Athena squeezed her eyes closed as a fresh wave of pain shot through her head.

She guessed she'd have to do the logical thing and exit the spaceship into the Sahara Desert's cousin and pray things didn't get worse.

The strong arms that surrounded her were enough to make her eyes fly open.

He was gripping her against him and she was very aware that all she was wearing was the soft, billowy wool-like material.

It took her by surprise but his skin felt a lot softer than it looked. It felt like suede moving over rock and Athena's cheeks grew warm from the proximity.

When was the last time she'd actually had some? Apparently way too long ago for her to be reacting like this!

He was an *alien*.

Her hormones apparently didn't mind that fact. It seemed as if her body was quite happy just having any male touch her, alien or not.

Well, maybe that was not entirely true. She had been grossed out by every other alien so far...

Just not so much by him.

Nevertheless, a mild wave of panic hit her as he raised her towards the hole he'd made in the roof. But the fact the hole was open and she wasn't starved of oxygen was enough proof she could breathe in the atmosphere.

How lucky. She shuddered to think what might have happened had things gone the other way.

"Your thin human skin is cold in this weather?" Xul frowned as he pushed her head through the opening and hoisted her upper body through the hole.

"I am not cold. Thank you very much."

Xul grunted.

Enough of her body was now through for her to grab onto the roof and help the rest of herself up. The little exertion made her breathless and Athena fell back to stare at the dull orange sky.

Ok, the first thing she needed to do when she returned to Earth was to start working out again.

If she made it back to Earth.

Looking around at the vast expanse of sand, there was nothing in view to tell her she'd be leaving this place very soon.

Something fell by her side and she realized he'd thrown up some sort of satchel. A frown furrowed her brow.

She hadn't seen him with that when they'd left.

Next, his hands gripped the sides of the hole and his horns appeared through the space as he hoisted himself up. Grunting at her as he pulled the rest of his body through, he reached down to grab his *sokja*—there was no way she was going to remember to call it that. 'Spear' would have to do.

He seemed to be paying her little attention as he fastened the satchel over his shoulders, grabbed his spear, and hopped off the top of the ship to land gracefully in the sand beneath him.

Pushing her head over the side of the ship, Athena eyed the distance. There was no way she was going to make it down without hurting herself and she was already in pain.

As if he understood that, Xul turned and looked up at her, his green eyes burning into hers.

"Are you coming or not?" he asked, causing Athena to frown.

"You don't really expect me to just jump into your arms after I just watched you kill a man, erm, thing, do you?"

"High Tasqals don't deserve the gift of life. Their crimes are too many." Xul blinked, as if his explanation was enough and he was waiting for her to jump. After a few moments, he raised an eyebrow at her. Having seen him up close now, she wondered how he even managed to do that seeing that his horns seemed to grow out of the same bone as his forehead.

"Suit yourself," he said and turned to leave.

"Wait!" Athena bit her bottom lip, weighing her options as she watched him pause, his back turned to her.

She could either take her chances with him or she could take her chances by herself.

"I'll come with you," she said, watching him cock his head to the side as he turned to look at her, slight amusement once again on his face.

He was playing with her. He knew she wouldn't let him leave without her.

Narrowing her eyes at him, Athena slipped her legs over the side of the ship, trying to judge the height. It wasn't a far drop. She could probably make it without his help. But she didn't have time to contemplate it further as Xul took a step forward, grasped her around the waist, and lifted her off the ship.

When he put her down, Athena could feel the warmth in her cheeks again. The last time she'd been manhandled like that was a long time ago. Her hormones loved it. The only problem was they shouldn't be acting up in a situation like this and they should realize that she hadn't been manhandled—she'd been bull-handled...devil-handled?

A loud rip caught her attention and she watched as he tore a piece of the corner of his loincloth to create one long strip.

"Your skull is bleeding," he said as he eyed her.

Raising a hand to the spot that ached, she realized he was right.

Wow, she must be really out of it to not have realized that before. No wonder her head was throbbing so much. It didn't explain the neck pain though. She just assumed that it was a case of whiplash... very bad whiplash.

Before she could protest, Xul wrapped the cloth around her head, covering the wound tightly.

Athena opened her mouth to mention that using a piece of cloth that spent its time hanging near his dick wasn't probably the most hygienic of things to use but the thought of mentioning that specific body part only made her cheeks grow warm again.

Did his dick look like a human's?

He looked similar enough to a human male for it to be possible.

Xul made a sound, almost like he was clearing his throat and Athena was sure her cheeks grew redder.

She'd been staring. Staring at his...area...and he'd caught her doing it.

She wasn't going to look up at him because she was sure what she would see on his face—that arrogant, slightly amused look.

Slipping something from his satchel, some kind of round gadget with several dials, Xul took a few seconds looking at it before turning to his left.

"This way," he said, then began moving.

The sand was already growing warm under her feet, even though the suns hadn't risen fully yet. Suns.

Two suns.

If that wasn't indication enough that she was far away from Earth then she didn't know what was.

As they walked, Athena had her eyes fixed on his back. His brown, thick mane flowed down his shoulders, covering his neck and she wondered what other surprises he had hiding behind there.

"Why did you kill it?" She blurted.

Xul didn't answer but she was positive he'd heard her.

"Don't you think I deserve to know?"

"No," he answered, and Athena felt her brows dive deep.

"Wouldn't you want to know why one of your enemies kills your other enemy?"

That caused him to stop and she almost bumped into his back.

He turned on her then, his eyes unreadable.

"I am not your enemy."

Athena blinked a few times. He sounded genuine and, to be honest, he really hadn't done anything to make her feel like he was out to harm her. He'd cut a piece of his clothes to bandage her head, for Pete's sake.

Still...

Then the thought occurred to her that he might have killed the High Tasqal to save her from being its slave. Ridiculous as it sounded, even to her, what other explanation was there?

"You killed him to save me?"

Xul's eyebrows rose and a hint of a smile crossed over his lips. "No," he said and turned to continue walking.

Without thinking about it, Athena grabbed onto his arm. His silky suede skin felt warm to the touch and they both looked down at her pale skin against his brown fur.

Pulling her hand away quickly, Athena hurriedly continued, "Why did you kill him?"

Xul narrowed his eyes and regarded her for a few seconds. "Of all the humans, you are the strangest one," he murmured.

She couldn't help but feel self-conscious about that. What did he mean by all the humans? What was so different between her and the others?

Hands akimbo, she frowned up at him. He kept calling her strange, yet *he* was the strange one.

"What makes me so different?"

"All the others have colorful manes. You do not."

If she remembered clearly, Song's hair was black. The thought of the other women made her wonder how they were getting on up there on that big ship. Would she even ever see them again?

Frowning up at Xul, she answered him. "One of them had black hair. That's not colorful."

She didn't even know why they were having this conversation. Surely, there were more important things to discuss like, let's say, where the hell he was going with such purpose.

"Yes, but she was small. You are all small. But she was noticeably so." He narrowed his eyes and reached forward to grasp her chin.

Athena found she could not move away, or maybe it was her mind that remained transfixed on him.

"Your features are...bland. No identifying horns. Is this how all humans look?"

In one movement, Athena slapped away his hand and a surprised look crossed over his features.

"That's not answering my question. You killed a man...a thing. You killed a thing. Right in front of me. You just popped out a knife from God knows where and lodged it in its throat." A shudder ran through her at the thought. The memory was fresh and she reckoned it would have been even more jarring if she'd seen something like that happen on Earth.

Thank God the aliens all looked like elements of her imagination. She could disassociate from it much more easily because of that.

"If you must know, I will tell you, human," Xul answered.

Finally, some progress.

She swore, he was as stubborn as a bull.

The irony wasn't lost on her but at least they were getting somewhere. Now, to get him to stop referring to her as 'human' every few minutes. It was demeaning.

"Athena," she said. "My name is Athena."

10

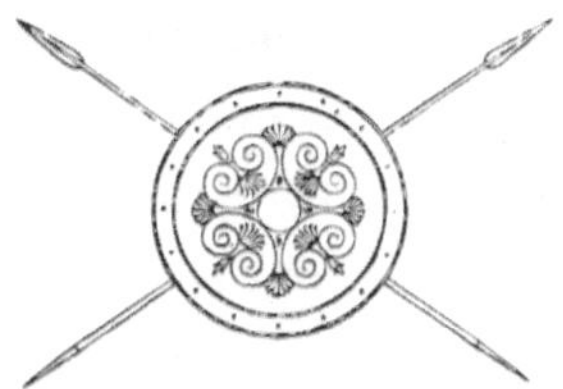

Xul lifted the spear from the sand and resumed walking.

"Ulruq," he glanced behind him to see if she was following, "the High Tasqal that bought you, was the leader of an underground ring dealing in illegal slaves, bought and sold for sex and breeding.

"The Tasqal species is dying out. Their species is diseased. Their flesh is covered in boils that start developing at the age of sexual readiness," he said, pausing to glance behind him again.

"You mean puberty?"

"We do not have that word in my tongue," Xul answered.

"It's puberty. Sexual readiness just makes it sound so, I don't know, dirty."

Xul raised an eyebrow. "Humans think sexual readiness is filth?"

"Yes. I mean, no," Athena shook her head to clear her thoughts. "Listen, let's not argue over semantics at the moment. Continue your story."

Xul frowned but continued. "The Tasqals are dying, so they have been moving from planet to planet spreading their diseased seed."

"Ugh." Athena made a face. "You really have a way of describing things."

Xul frowned again as if he did not understand what she meant.

"Go on, never mind me." Athena motioned to him before pointing her gaze to the footprints he was leaving in the sand. She was stepping directly in the ones he made and his feet were gigantic compared to hers.

She'd noticed earlier that his feet were also a lot more suited to walking barefooted than hers were. His seemed to have hardened skin on the sole that was bound to come in handy later. Her feet, on the other hand, were already starting to burn up from the hot sand.

"The boils they carry are contagious. Their young that grow within the other species contaminates. Entire worlds have died because of their scourge." She could hear that the last words came out through gritted teeth and she wondered if his world was one of the ones destroyed. But he didn't give her a chance to ask, as he continued.

"They do not care who they mate with. Wives. Mothers." He paused. "Female young."

Athena's eyes widened.

Surely, he could not mean...

"Are you referring to female children?" When Xul didn't answer she knew she was right.

"They are scum," he finally said. "My alliance sent me undercover to take out the leader. It was the first phase of our operation."

"Wait, what operation? You're a soldier?"

"No," he said before turning to glance at her. "I am a rebel."

It was Athena's turn to raise an eyebrow.

Well, well, well. Maybe she had walked into the Star Wars universe after all.

THEY'D BEEN WALKING for what felt like hours now; their footprints spread a long line marking their path behind them.

The wreckage from the ship was now just a little dot on the horizon and the twin suns were moving high in the sky.

Athena staggered behind. Her throat was burning, her head was throbbing, and it felt like the skin was stripping off her feet.

Xul was a few steps in front of her and, as the minutes ticked by, the gap between them grew larger and larger.

"Hey," she called out to him, noting that her voice sounded much weaker than before.

Xul paused and turned to look at her.

"Mind telling me where you're going? Is there even anything in this wilderness?" She was panting by the time she caught up with him.

"We are heading to the Muk outpost. It is five more days' travel."

Five more days? She couldn't continue like this for five more days.

"I can't walk like this for five more days," she breathed.

Xul took a moment to look at her thoughtfully.

"I was right. Your presence will be a problem," he finally said.

Athena frowned. She didn't have a lot of energy but she had enough to glare at him.

"Excuse me, but I didn't ask to be kidnapped," she snapped. "Twice at that. Why did you not abort your plan then if you had already figured I would be such a bother?"

Xul crossed his arms over his chest and the action only made him seem bigger.

"A chance to get so close to Ulruq doesn't come twice. I had to take the opportunity."

Athena huffed. "And what now? Don't you think they are going to come after us?"

"No," he said with such certainty, Athena's frown got deeper. "Muk is a harsh planet."

Athena rolled her eyes, pointing behind her at the trail of footprints they'd left from the ship right to the spot they were standing.

"Um, I know you say that but you still haven't made an effort to hide our location. If this Ulruq was so important, they are bound to come after him and they have a trail leading right to us."

Xul made to speak but Athena held up a hand, stopping him. "Not to mention, I really don't think I can continue much further like this."

Xul's green gaze washed over her and again she became very aware that she was wearing only the soft, billowy wool.

"A sandstorm is coming soon. We must take shelter and rest," he said.

Turning to look around them, she wondered if he was seeing something she wasn't.

"Take shelter?" She gestured around them. "Where?"

Walking a few steps away from her, Xul approached what looked like a small sand dune. She called it small but it was as tall as he was and twice as wide—which meant it was much bigger than she was.

Raising his spear in the air, he punctured the sand in one movement, driving the spear deep.

Athena was about to ask him if he had gone mad when the sand began to shake. Xul pulled out his spear and raised it again, poised to strike.

As the sand shook, something reared from beneath it with a loud sound like tree bark stretching.

"Stand back!" Xul shouted.

She didn't need to hear twice, she was already stumbling backward.

Something big came up through the sand and between the dust and chaos, Athena could hardly see Xul.

One moment, she saw that he was repeatedly stabbing his spear into the thing's stalk. Next, the sound of tree bark crashing to the ground reached Athena's ears.

Coughing on the disturbed sand that made it hard for her to breathe, she waited for the sand to settle.

When she was finally able to see the scene in front of her, her eyes widened.

"What the actual hell?"

What she saw in front of her looked like a giant Venus flytrap mated with a woolly mammoth. It had a long stalk that extended several meters into the air. The Venus flytrap part was covered in thick dark strands of hair on the outside and there were spiky thorns along the edges.

Xul speared it again and the thing gave one last twitch.

"What the hell is that?"

Xul glanced up at her before proceeding to slice the flytrap section off the stalk.

"Shelter," he said.

Ooookay then. Athena glanced around her, counting the number of dunes that she saw in their proximity.

"Do these um," she pointed to the dunes before wrapping her arms around herself, "do these all have those things in them?"

Even from where she stood she could see the slight amusement on his face. She was happy he was having such a fun time. Resisting the urge to scowl at him, she waited for his answer.

"Yes," he said, "every lump is a resting zehmip."

Athena scowled then. "Hey buddy," she stalked over to him, carefully stepping over the long decapitated stalk of the zehmip, "mind letting me know something like that sooner? What if I had disturbed one?"

"Then I would have killed it," Xul replied but his matter-of-fact tone only made her want to slap him.

Hauling the head to an area away from the other dunes, Xul planted the thorny bits deep into the sand to make a tent-like shape. As he returned to her position, he chopped the stalk into two sections, the larger of which he split again.

When he hauled the two pieces back to the 'tent,' he sliced them into thin strips and stuck them into the sand to make what looked like makeshift doors or, rather, barriers.

Athena watched him work, feeling what was left of her energy draining by the second.

The wind was picking up and it did seem like a storm was heading their way.

The only thing that was keeping her standing was the fact that there would potentially be someplace better to rest than in the scorching sun. The shade of the tent looked inviting.

Using his spear to slice the remaining section into small bits, Xul motioned to the tent.

"You should enter. The storm will be sudden and harsh," he said.

Moving the barrier, Xul allowed her to enter the tent.

Athena paused for only a second. Climbing in under what was essentially the mouth of the zehmip felt dangerous but not as much as it would have felt like if the thing was still alive.

Gulping as she settled on the warm sand underneath, she breathed out a sigh. The shade was a godsend. Her feet were aching and her throat was dry.

She needed to find water soon. And food. She needed to find food.

She couldn't remember the last time she'd eaten. That would have been on Earth, probably after she'd fed her dog, Magnet.

As her mind ran on the dog again, she felt a sense of loss and longing.

Would she ever see him again?

Would she ever see Earth again?

Hiding the worry behind her eyes, she watched as Xul climbed in under the tent.

With his big frame under the zehmip, the space suddenly felt too small.

"So I guess we're sharing," Athena murmured. Not that she minded. She was certainly thankful for all he'd done so far.

Killing her captor.

Taking her on a wild trek through a barren land with sneaky giant man-eating plants.

You know. The usual things that happened when you've just met someone.

"We sleep now. Travel at night," Xul said as he crawled in and settled beside her.

Athena glanced at their shoulders barely touching before moving her eyes swiftly to his face.

He didn't seem to mind.

Damn.

She'd touched an alien.

Many times now.

The thought was...mind-blowing.

"Wouldn't it be more dangerous to travel at night?"

He glanced at her, an eyebrow raised. "Your planet has not discovered much of the universe as yet, I suppose," he mused.

Athena narrowed her eyes. Somehow, she felt the need to defend Earth but what should she say?

He was right.

To most people on Earth, people like him only existed in movies.

"The creatures of Muk are alive in the night. The zehmips raise their heads and feast on anything unlucky to get too close and the sand cats hunt for food for their young."

He must have taken her shocked silence for her wanting him to continue because he went on. "The daytime is the only time the land is not teeming with life. Only sandstorms and sand twists," he said.

"Sand twists?" Athena frowned, trying to imagine what that looked like.

"A column of twisting air that goes high in the air," Xul frowned as if she should know what a sand twist was.

"Ohh, you mean like a tornado? Wait, there are tornados here too?" Athena groaned.

"If that is what you call them in your language," he said.

"Is there no place in outer space that is safe?" Athena groaned again. "It's literally been hell since I've gotten here. Not exactly a tourist brochure, is it?"

A low rumble sounded in Xul's throat and a glance told her he was amused again.

Rolling her eyes, she lay down and turned her back to him.

"Sleep," he said. "We walk when night falls."

Well, judging from when she'd last looked up into the sky, it must be close to noon if this planet moved around its suns at a similar speed to Earth.

"What happens after we get to your outpost?" Athena rubbed her nose as she spoke. The zehmip had a funny scent, almost like coal.

"I will send the signal for a pickup," Xul murmured, obviously more focused on whatever he was doing that she could not see.

"And what about me? Where do I fit into this grand plan of yours?"

"That's the problem," Xul said. "You weren't a part of the plan."

11

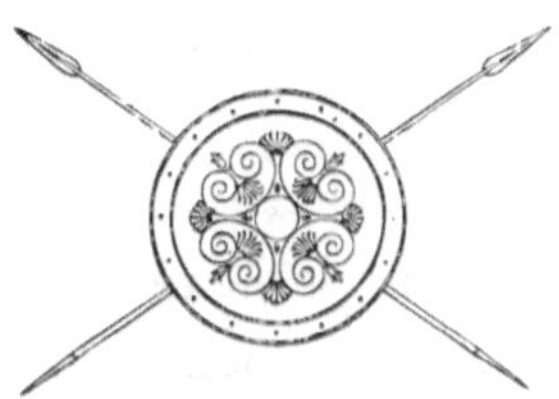

That was exactly what a girl wanted to hear when she was literally in the middle of God knows where with no idea how to get home.

Spinning around to face him, Athena glared up at his large form.

"And where exactly is this pickup going to take you?"

"Back to where we started. The Isclit's ship."

"Oh, no, no, no. Why are you heading back there?! Surely, you want to get far away. You just killed one of their leaders!"

"The rest of the Restitution will be attacking other similar ships soon. It is my duty to fight."

Athena took a moment to digest that news.

"So, there will be a combined war effort in a few days, and you want to head towards it, not away from it."

Xul glanced at her over his shoulder, his green-eyed gaze catching hers and holding it there.

"It is my duty," he said.

Athena released a breath and turned her back again.

But the more she thought about it, the more the idea of going back to the Isclit ship made sense. If they did, maybe she could help the other women escape. She wondered what they were going through. She wouldn't say she was having it relatively easy but she imagined that back on the ship it was much worse.

"What happens after the war?" She was so tired now, she barely had the energy to put any strength in her voice and her words came out in a soft whisper.

"Then the Restitution will regroup."

"And what about us? What happens to all the slaves and animals that were abducted?"

"You can go to the interplanetary hub and send a message to your home planet for pickup."

That was enough for her to sit upright.

"You mean we can send a message to Earth?"

"If that is what you wish, the facility is there," Xul said. He was busy gutting the center of the stalk that he'd cut into small pieces.

A thrill of hope went through her and Athena smiled at him for the first time.

"Thank you," she whispered.

Xul turned to glance back at her and paused, his eyes running over her face. Nodding slightly, he turned back to his work.

Athena stared into the slight pink tinge of the zehmip's mouth. Stretching her hand outward, she ran her fingers along the surprisingly soft interior. She could feel the warmth emanating from the outside and felt a wave of relief that she was no longer walking out underneath the suns. Her feet were still aching but she hadn't the strength to look at them.

Maybe in the morning, or night rather, when they would get up again and start their trek.

Athena sighed, anticipation in her veins.

There was a chance to be saved. Not only for her but the other women who'd been captured as well.

Thinking of walking five more days didn't seem so bad knowing there was hope in sight.

Xul had his back turned to Athena but he was alert to her every move.

The female human's presence was unnerving in a sort of way that he could not describe.

She had turned away from him and was tracing patterns against the inside cheek of the zehmip. He wondered what she was thinking.

Glancing at the zehmip stalk in his hand, he continued gutting out the soft yellow flesh. He didn't know how she was going to take it but this was going to be their food and drink for the day ahead.

The zehmip's meat was both energy-dense and had a high fluid content. It would stop them from starving to death and keep them hydrated in the wilderness of Muk.

As he finished scooping the last of the flesh from the plant, Xul cut thin strips from the bark. Those he used to wrap around the scooped out flesh.

He was done in a few minutes and his eyes fell on the little barriers he'd made. In the night, those barriers would not stand up to the sand cats that were bound to come into the tent, looking for food for their young.

They were large beasts that slept in their dens under the sand in the day but came out to hunt at night. As a matter of fact, they looked much like the beast the Isclits had removed from the humans' terrarium, except the sand cats had much larger ears, no protruding teeth, and were the exact color of the sand underneath which they lived. They were elusive creatures, however, always choosing sneaky approaches when hunting their prey and they always hunted in groups.

He would have to keep a sharp eye as they trekked toward the outpost as he was sure the human, Athena, had no idea what was in store out there in the wilderness. And there was no time to teach her about it.

As the wind picked up, another sound caught his ears.

It was a soft sound, almost inaudible, but his ears were highly sensitive and the sound floated into them easily.

Turning to look behind him, he watched her shoulders rise and fall in a slow rhythm. Frowning, he leaned closer, his eyebrows shooting up as he realized she was indeed doing what he thought she was.

She was sleeping.

Either she was entirely comfortable in his presence or she was so tired from the ordeal that her body had gone into maintenance mode.

Either way, it was the perfect opportunity for him to observe her more closely.

The entire time they'd been walking, he'd been waiting to hear her complain about the journey. Yet, she hadn't. Not until he himself had been thinking about taking a break.

Peculiar creature, she was.

Moving closer, he studied her face.

She had pouty little pink lips and a small defiant chin. Her skin was soft and hairless, offering no protection to the elements. As Xul found himself moving closer, his leg brushed against her foot and she winced in her sleep.

Xul frowned, his eyes flashing to her feet. Gently taking one into his hands, he marveled at how small they were.

It was a wonder she was even able to carry her body weight on such small and, once again, delicate, things.

She hadn't complained, but he didn't need to be a human doctor to know that something was wrong with them. She had no pads underneath her feet to protect them from anything.

Anything sharp could easily puncture the soft skin. His brows furrowed deeper.

He imagined walking on the hot sand was also painful, and if the redness and blisters along her heel and sole were any indication, the harsh sand of Muk was already taking a toll on her.

Cursing underneath his breath, he rested her foot back against the sand.

The human's Earth must be highly safe and without hazards. How else could the human species survive if they were so easily wounded?

With one last glance at her, Xul grabbed his spear and crept from the tent, making sure he did not wake her.

SOMETHING ROUSED her from her sleep, Athena wasn't sure what but she didn't need to glance around the tent to realize she was alone.

Xul's large presence no longer overpowered the space and that made her sit upright too quickly, causing a new pounding in her head.

Hand placed lightly over the bandaged wound, as if that would help with the pain, Athena squinted.

Something like a high whistle split through the air again, and Athena froze. That's the sound that woke her but she had no idea what it was. As the sides of their makeshift tent shook, she could only assume that it was the wind.

If not, it was some animal and she needed to protect herself.

Trying to see outside, she peeked through a narrow space in one of the barriers.

All she could see was brown, in the air and on the ground.

Sand was swirling all around them. The storm was picking up.

Well...the sand was swirling all around her, for she was alone.

A feeling of dread grew in her stomach. His spear was gone and at one side of the tent, he'd placed some neatly wrapped packages. Were those packets food?

Athena settled back on her haunches as she stared at the little packages, putting two and two together.

He'd left her, hadn't he?

Maybe he'd thought that she was going to be too much trouble on his journey or maybe he just didn't like her company.

She'd tried really hard not to complain while they were walking, even though the sand was so coarse it had easily grated on her feet, creating blisters.

But she'd kept her mouth shut.

It had been either follow him or take her chances and return to the wreckage—and the latter option wasn't really an option.

As she pulled her knees up to herself, Athena sighed and tried to think positively.

So what if he'd left her? She'd survived this long; surely she could survive a little longer.

He'd told her enough to let her know that she should stay awake at nighttime and sleep during the days.

She could use this tent as her outpost and try to find food. If there were plants on Muk then there must be water somewhere. She just had to find it.

It would be just like Girl Scouts...just solo and way more dangerous.

She had no choice.

She could do this.

But even as she repeated the mantra to herself, she couldn't help the feeling of dread that was enveloping her soul.

Placing her forehead on her knees, Athena squeezed her eyes shut.

She wasn't going to cry. She wasn't.

She'd maintained her composure for so long, even after waking up in a cell with aliens, even after being chased by a frickin' saber-toothed tiger, even after being auctioned, even after her 'owner' made it very clear what he planned to do with her when they reached his ship...heck, even after watching an assassination in live and living color and then crash-landing on a desert planet.

She. Was. Not. Going. To. Cry.

Yet, the thought that Xul had left her made everything seem worse. Maybe it was because, out of all of this, he was the only alien she'd met that was even mildly nice.

She must admit he was a bit difficult to deal with but not so much so that she wasn't getting used to him.

Or maybe it was the fact that he'd suddenly dropped the bomb that there was a chance she could return to Earth.

Why drop that bomb and then leave?

He represented that hope, and now it seemed as if he was gone.

12

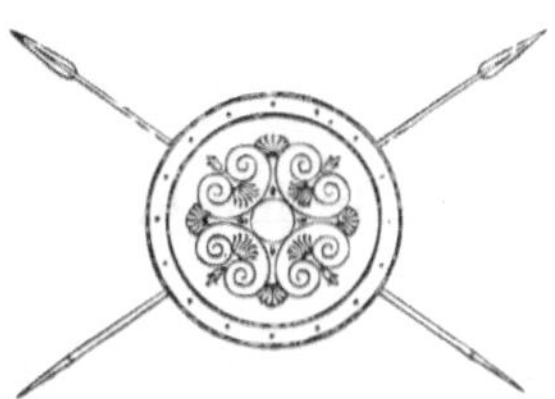

It was worse now, the wind, howling incessantly and shaking the little tent. Athena was curled up in the center of the tent, listening to the wind howl and each howl and whistle seemed to take with it a bit of her resolve.

There was so much sand in the air now, the light from the suns was completely blocked out and it seemed like night outside. She wondered whether that meant the creatures that lived on Muk were going to leave their little hidey-holes. She needed one problem at a time. She could deal with that. What she couldn't deal with was a series of problems, one after the other, with no resolution in sight.

A section of the barrier moved and that made her jump. Scrambling backward, she stared at the barrier.

If there were weapons close by she would have been scrambling to get one. But there was nothing in the tent. Nothing except those weird little wrapped packages Xul had left. She'd investigated them before and the smell was foul.

Maybe she'd been wrong about him leaving them for food. And now that she thought about it, why would he have gone through the trouble to leave her food anyway?

Her chances of survival on her own were already dim.

But she wasn't going to give up.

Gripping the only thing she could use for defense, Athena dug her fingers into the sand and took up two handfuls.

Maybe she could throw it into the face of whatever it was that was trying to get in, momentarily stunning them, and then she could dash out the other exit and into...well, let's not think about that yet. One problem at a time, remember?

The barrier popped open and in came the horns then the body of a large beas—no, it was Xul.

But it was already too late, her reflexes were too fast. The two handfuls of sand were already hurtling through the air to land squarely on his forehead.

Xul paused, took a moment to secure the barrier for sand was getting inside the tent, then turned to glare at her.

Athena's hands flew over her mouth. "I'm sorry. I thought you were a predator."

Xul's eyes narrowed as he bent his head to shake off the sand then raised an eyebrow at Athena.

For a moment, he just looked at her and then a rumble left his chest as he threw his head back and laughed.

It was a wonderful deep sound that made her insides tingle and it was Athena's turn to frown. Ignoring the tingle, she focused on the obvious thing in front of her.

He was laughing at her.

"I'm glad you find that so funny."

"You think sand will stop a predator?" His laughter was replaced by a grin now and Athena tried to ignore the pull of that surprisingly attractive smile.

It was like one of those grins you wished that hot guy in high school would direct your way. You know, the one that made girls swoon in the hallway. Yep, that same one that created groupies all yearning to have that title of being his girlfriend.

Athena frowned deeper. What was wrong with her?

Xul was an alien. Nothing was going to change that.

Sure, he was tall, and strong...her eyes ran over his shoulders and chest, pausing at his loincloth.

And sure, he looked much like a ripped male human, only bigger and with horns.

And sure, remove the fact that if he wasn't an alien, she would probably be drooling over him...

That all didn't mean anything.

He was an alien.

And, so far, she'd found out the hard way that most aliens were full of shit.

And what was he doing here anyway? She thought he'd left her to fend for herself.

Xul's grin slowly disappeared as he regarded her but the amusement didn't leave his eyes.

"Sand was all I had after you left." Athena tried to keep her voice level. She wasn't quite sure if she should be happy or angry at the moment.

Xul grunted, dropping to his knees in front of her. Resting his spear, he reached for her foot.

Athena pulled it out of his reach immediately.

"There's something called boundaries you know." She frowned then eyed him. "What are you doing anyway?"

"Your feet need healing," he said, outstretching his hand again.

"And you're going to heal them?" Athena raised an eyebrow. "How?"

"Give me your foot." He reached for her foot again and Athena reluctantly let him take it.

His touch wasn't soft but judging from how he'd ripped open the ship and taken down the zehmip, he was trying to be really gentle with her.

Reaching into his sack, he pulled out what looked like a purplish flower.

"What's that?"

"It's an herb. It will make you feel better."

Athena watched him work. Squeezing the flower, he let the little drops of fluid that came from it fall on her sole.

"You went to get that for me?"

Xul glanced up at her and something passed behind his eyes before he blinked. "I do not need you lagging behind when we trek tonight."

Athena frowned at his cold answer but did not respond. There was no use arguing with him. For now, she'd just accept his kindness without protest until she knew enough to start fending for herself.

They had a long trek ahead of them. She was pretty sure she was going to need to get more of the flowers he'd found and keep them around.

The fluid from the petals was already soothing the blisters and Athena eyed him as he worked. How did he even know about these things?

When he finished, Xul put her feet down and grabbed one of the packages he'd wrapped and set to the side.

Glancing at her, he put one by her legs and proceeded to unwrap his. It only took him a few seconds before the yellow meat of the zehmip was in his mouth and he was chewing. His eyes narrowed as he watched her.

Grasping the package he'd put down for her, she lifted it to her nose and was instantly repelled.

"Oh shit." She held the thing far from her nose. "Oh God, this reeks!"

Xul's eyes were still narrowed. "It is not dung," he said. "And, as I said before, spirits don't answer prayers in this place."

Athena blinked then tried hard to hold back the laugh that threatened at her lips. "'Oh shit' is an Earth phrase. It's just something you say when something negative happens or if you're surprised. And I'm not literally calling on God himself when I say oh God...it's just an expression."

Xul's eyes narrowed some more.

Yes, yes. She knew what he was thinking. Humans are peculiar and yada yada.

Sniffing the package again, she tried not to puke. The thing did smell vile.

"You're sure this is food? It smells like something you leave to kill your enemies, not something you willfully ingest."

Xul snorted softly. "Eat. You will need the strength for tonight." He took another portion of his into his mouth and Athena screwed up her nose.

"Eat," he pressed. "Then we will sleep."

As the traitor that it was, her stomach chose to growl at that very moment. Reluctantly, Athena opened the package and looked at the contents.

The zehmip's flesh looked nothing like it smelled and that was probably for the best. As she took another sniff, she could feel Xul watching her but she paid him no attention. Using her fingers to pin her nose, she tipped her head back and let some of the zehmip's flesh fall into her mouth.

It was soft and somewhat sticky and every chew released a burst of sweet fluid. If you got past the fact that it smelled like dirty socks, it wasn't so bad. Chewing quickly, she took some more into her mouth, pinned her nose, and repeated the process.

She was finished after repeating the process eight more times and when she was done, she noticed Xul was studying her with his usual amused expression.

"For someone who complains that something smells like dung, you ate it very quickly," he murmured.

Athena opened her mouth to answer him but the amusement growing in his eyes made her realize he was only riling her up. "You know what, I am going to rest for the trek ahead." She said, turning her back to him as she reclined on the sand.

"So am I," Xul said, as he moved to lie beside her. They weren't touching, but she could feel his presence beside her.

Outside the tent, the wind howled, making the sides of the zehmip shake.

"Are you sure this thing will hold?" Athena asked. "It sounds really rough out there."

"This is a lesser storm," Xul replied. "We will be safe for the day."

Well, she'd have to take his word for it.

Hours later, the wind was still howling but Athena could not sleep. Her mind was on other things. Like the fact that not long ago she'd been back on Earth enjoying a relatively simple life and now she was cooped up in a tent in the middle of a desert planet, her only companion a burly alien.

Speaking of him, Athena glanced over her shoulder. He was lying on his back now but his eyes were closed. She assumed he was still sleeping.

How he managed to sleep when the wind was so loud outside, she did not know, but if what he'd said was anything to go by, she'd have to learn to do the same thing soon.

Gingerly outstretching a hand, she used a finger to touch his hair. It was a lot softer than she expected and Athena raised an eyebrow.

Either they had some really good conditioner on his planet or he had really good genes.

Judging from the soft fuzz covering the rest of his body, she was going to bet on the second one.

But that was where the softness stopped.

His face was hard and his chest too.

Leaning closer, she frowned as she investigated his horns.

They were coming directly out of his forehead and went up into the air, the ends pointed. She bet if he wanted to gore anybody, he could.

What else would they be there for? Surely the evolutionary purpose of the horns was for battle.

The horns looked like they were made of thick bone and they were both ribbed.

Stretching her hand further, she ran a finger down one of the horns when Xul's eyes snapped open.

A growl escaped his lips and then he was grabbing her wrist. In the next second, he was rolling over and pinning her underneath him.

It took a few seconds for his green gaze to focus on her surprised face and the snarl to leave his lips.

"What are you doing, human?" he grumbled.

Athena took a few deep breaths. The movement had been so sudden; it was like it had surprised the air out of her lungs. His body was pressed against hers, her arm pinned above her head, and Athena tried not to think about the fact that her breasts were heaving against his chest.

"I wasn't doing anything, alien." She put emphasis on the last word and watched him frown before he grunted. She was going to call him that for as long as he decided to refer to her only as "human."

"It is strange that you see *me* as the alien," he mused.

He was close. So, so close. His hot breath brushed over her face.

And for some reason she really could not describe, her wandering eyes fell from his gaze to fall on his lips.

When her eyes finally met his again, she realized he was studying her once more.

"You are interested in my horns." It was more of a statement than a question and Athena wondered if he needed her to answer.

When he remained silent as if waiting on her to say something, she jerked her head in a nod.

Releasing her wrist, Xul planted his hands on either side of her body.

"Your species does not have horns, yet you look similar to us," he mused.

"Well," Athena cleared her throat, very aware that she was still beneath him and he was making no effort to roll off. "We don't need horns for battle."

His eyebrows rose and he seemed amused by that.

"My horns are not used for battle," he said, his eyes searching her face.

Athena frowned. "Then what are they used for?"

"They are a symbol of my species' virility. The longer the horns, the bigger the—"

"Okay!" Athena raised her hand to stop him. She'd heard enough. There was no need for him to go on.

If he was trying to tell her he was packed down there, then mission accomplished, for his horns were very long and erm...thick.

Amusement flooded his gaze immediately. "They are also used by the women of my species as something to hold on to when they are being pleasured."

He must have seen the red rise in her cheeks because a deep chuckle rumbled through his chest, vibrating against her and filling their little tent with his laughter.

For a few seconds, Xul remained above her, staring down at her and she could almost see the thoughts flying behind his eyes.

His eyes fell to her lips and she saw him pause. Then, as if whatever thoughts he was having disturbed him, he promptly rolled off her, stood, and grabbed his spear.

Athena averted her gaze.

Thanks to his little lesson, every time she looked at his loincloth she was going to be wondering what was hiding behind it. And now, she had a good idea.

"We must move," Xul said, picking up the remainder of the food he'd packed and stuffing them into his satchel.

Around them, the wind was not howling as wildly as before but dusk was starting to set in.

In the next moment, Xul removed the barrier and stepped outside, before putting it back in place.

There was still sand swirling in the wind and Athena wondered how they were going to travel with the sand beating against them.

Maybe it would have been possible with some kind of covering, but with none, she didn't really see how it was going to work.

Glancing down at herself, she noticed that the soft-billowy wool seemed a lot smaller than it did just hours before.

Maybe it was her bad memory but it looked like it was shrinking.

Xul opened the barrier again and threw something hairy inside.

It looked suspiciously like the skin of the zehmip.

Closer inspection proved she was right.

Xul popped his head into the tent, his horns almost poking holes into the top.

"Put that over yourself. We move now," he said, eyeing her before exiting the tent again.

Athena looked over the hairy zehmip skin again.

It was thick, the underside smooth and the exterior having that woolly mammoth-type fur she'd noticed earlier.

Shrugging the thing over herself, it was just enough to cover her from her head to her thighs.

It wasn't perfect, but it would have to do.

Just then, Xul moved the barrier and popped his head in again, looking her up and down.

"Let's move," he said.

Athena nodded and exited the tent.

The first thing that hit her was the wind.

Minute grains of sand stung her face as they beat against her skin.

Pulling the makeshift zehmip coat higher to protect her face, she realized that she wouldn't be able to see anything with the storm still blowing around them.

"I can't see anything!" she shouted, mildly aware that Xul was standing somewhere close by.

Through her restricted vision, she saw that he, too, had a zehmip coat pulled over himself to protect against the flying sand.

He was checking his compass device to figure out which direction to head in.

"I can't see anything!" Athena repeated, pressing against the wind to get closer to Xul's large form.

He turned to her and said something, but the wind took his words away.

Pushing something long and narrow in her hand, she realized he was handing her a piece of the zehmip stalk. She was mildly confused until she felt him tug against it.

It was a lead.

She'd have to hold on to it so she didn't get lost.

Apparently satisfied that she was holding on to the thing, Xul began moving forward and Athena followed behind.

The sand was deep and loose, making her feet sink with every step. She couldn't see anything in front of her, all that was there was swirling sand and darkness was setting in.

Coupled with the wind pressing against her, the only thing that felt sure and secure was the zehmip stalk she was holding on to.

The constant soft pull was a reminder that she was not alone.

An alien was on the other end and though that would have terrified her a day before, it was comforting at that moment.

Athena settled on that thought as she gripped the stalk for dear life.

Right now, it was her only connection to freedom and probably even survival.

13

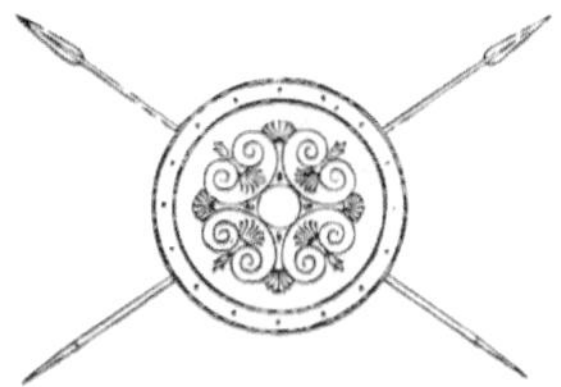

The human was keeping up.

Xul pulled on the stalk every now and again to make sure she was still there.

He couldn't see her in the swirling of the sand, neither could he hear if she called him.

Pulling the coat of the zehmip further over himself, he brought the compass closer to his face so he could check if he was heading in the right direction.

If he'd been traveling alone, it would have been much easier. He'd be making much more progress. But he couldn't dwell on that now. The fact was that she was there, whether he liked it or not.

As the former commander used to say, missions never went to plan. It was up to the soldier to adapt and fulfill his mission.

They had only a few days to traverse Muk, reach the outpost, and make contact.

For now, that was his mission, and it was one he was going to fulfill.

The lives of too many people depended on his success—not only the lives of the slaves on board, but those of his men as well.

Pulling lightly on the zehmip stalk, he felt the slight resistance on the other end and a soft smile smoothed his lips.

They had been walking for about two hours and night was upon them but she hadn't complained...not that he could hear her anyway.

But he assumed that if she wanted to stop she'd have stopped walking.

Closing his eyes for a few seconds, he tried to empty his mind and concentrate.

One of his men, Yce, was on board and if he could focus enough, maybe he could contact him. Yce's powers were still something he didn't quite understand but the soldier had the unique ability to connect minds and transfer information.

His skill had been useful on many a mission and Xul wouldn't be surprised if Yce was going to prove useful on this mission as well.

But he couldn't connect with him. Maybe it was the storm interfering, or maybe he was just too far away.

He doubted it was the second one, though. Yce had been known to connect with people of his kind many galaxies away.

Pressing against the wind, Xul gave the zehmip stalk another light tug and froze when he felt no resistance.

One more tug and he pulled the stalk right towards him, the other end reaching him with no human attached.

"Qrak," he cursed underneath his breath, moving into action immediately.

"Human!" he called, but his voice was lost in the wind. Retracing his steps, he tried to catch a glimpse of the female's small body anywhere but he could not see her. Even with his enhanced vision, the swirling sand was making it difficult to see anything around him.

Qrak, qrak, qrak.

And then he heard it. The undeniable growl of a sand cat.

Only, sand cats never hunted alone. They always hunted in groups of no less than five.

Spear raised, Xul squinted as he tried to see through the sand, his heart beating in his chest.

If sand cats were close, he needed to find the human, and he needed to find her fast.

***

ATHENA OPENED her mouth to scream but it was only filled with sand.

Something was gripping her and pulling her backward, away from the stalk and away from Xul.

The pain that shot up her right leg possibly meant that whatever was pulling her backward had also sunk its teeth deep into her leg.

Coughing out the sand in her mouth, she squinted against the sand in the air and dug her fingers into the sand beneath her.

Fucking sand everywhere. Curse this damn planet.

There was no grip.

Fuck!

Even with her fingers dug deep into the sand, it was not stopping the thing from pulling her backward.

Kicking behind her with her one good leg, she kicked into the air. Correcting the trajectory, she aimed and kicked again.

This time, her foot connected with something big, hard, and furry.

Aiming again, she put as much power as she could into the kick and landed a second blow.

The thing growled for the first time, and a chill ran down Athena's spine.

It sounded like a lion. Probably even bigger.

The thing twisted her, causing pain to shoot up her leg, and suddenly she was being pulled on her back.

Even with the sand swirling around them, she could feel the blood running down her right leg. She still couldn't see a thing but she did the only thing she could do and rained down kicks into the thing's head.

Pulling the zehmip cloak over her face to stop the sand, she shouted Xul's name, but she was sure he was either too far away by now or he hadn't even realized she was no longer holding the stalk.

Kicking as hard as she could again, her foot landed into something soft and she hoped it was the thing's eye. It growled again and threw her to the side, dropping her leg in the process.

Athena scrambled backward, her heart beating hard in her chest.

She knew it was going to come after her again soon and she had nothing to defend herself with.

As she scrambled backward, her back hit something hard. At first, she thought it was a rock, but the soft sand that fell from the contact told her it was something else.

It was one of those sleeping Venus trap things.

A growl somewhere beside her reached her ears and Athena scrambled on top of the dune.

The wind was starting to ease but it was still not low enough for her to see clearly or even shout loud enough to be heard.

As she scrambled on top of the dune, a slight movement underneath the sand made her heart beat in her throat.

Fuck. She was trading one predator for another but she would just have to take her chances.

Zehmips hunted for food using their flytrap mouths. If she avoided the mouth, she should be safe.

Another loud growl sounded somewhere to her left and Athena swallowed hard, pulling herself as high as she could on top of the dune.

Her injured leg was limp and useless, so she only had one leg to work with, but she was going to climb to the top if it was the last thing she did.

And she prayed it wasn't the last thing she did.

There was another growl, this time on her right, and Athena dug her hands deeper into the sand and tried to pull herself up higher.

It sounded like there was more than one.

As the wind slowed a little more and Athena could see a bit better, her fear gave her a fresh burst of energy.

In the darkness, twelve glowing eyes followed her movements and they were all surrounding the dune.

A sound behind her made her look back and her eyes widened a little as she saw two of the eyes jump on top of the dune. Whatever it was, it was climbing up the dune toward her.

She was almost at the top now, but if the things could climb, what was she going to do then?

As another pounced on the dune and began climbing upwards, Athena's mind fired off scenarios in her head.

There was only one thing she could do now.

Without thinking twice, she dug her hands deep into the sand, praying that she was nowhere near the mouth of the zehmip.

Her arm was almost completely subdued in the sand when she felt something hairy under her fingers.

Bingo!

Feeling along the hair, she pushed her arm further underneath the sand as she watched the glowing eyes move closer and closer to her.

To her right, another pair of glowing eyes jumped onto the dune and stalked closer.

Athena gulped, her hand searching underneath the sand for the right spot. But the sand was deep and she had to trust her instincts.

One of the creatures pounced and gripped on to the wool-like material she had wrapped around her waist.

It pulled it off her but the material got stuck in its mouth.

Its mild confusion bought her more time.

Lifting her leg again, she gave the beast a harsh kick that sent it flying off the dune.

From what she could see, the thing was long and big, like a skinny lion with large pointed ears like a fruit bat.

Another one jumped on the dune and Athena gritted her teeth, her hand underneath the sand desperately searching for what she was looking for.

As the wind died down a little more, she heard a shout in the distance.

Xul.

The sound of his voice gave her a little more hope but he was still far away or maybe he couldn't see her.

She needed to find the zehmip's mouth or she would be over in a few seconds.

As the golden eyes of one of the predators drew closer, it crouched low on its front legs and made to pounce on her.

In that second, Athena found what she was looking for.

Fingers closing around one of the thorns on the zehmip's mouth, she yanked as hard as she could and held on.

The rumbling underneath the sand was immediate and the predators yelped.

The sound of tree bark stretching filled the air and then she was being lifted high above the ground.

With the wind dying around her, she saw as the glowing eyes fell to the ground beneath her.

Spinning around to face the zehmip, she realized she was hanging on to the top of its head. Its mouth was open and she grabbed another one of its thorns.

In a movement too fast for her to comprehend, the zehmip dipped its head and tried to snap at one of the large cat-like creatures. It missed as the creature dashed out of the way. But that didn't stop it from swooping again.

Athena closed her eyes for a second. She was getting dizzy. It was like being on the 200-foot drop at Six Flags.

As the zehmip swooped again, this time it caught one of the cats in its mouth and its jaws slammed shut immediately.

Beneath her, she felt the animal's desperate attempts to escape from its impending death as it clawed against the zehmip's jaw. But there was nowhere for it to go. It was going to be digested. Athena tried to withhold the sudden urge to puke and concentrated on what was happening below her.

There was the shadowy figure of a man with horns attacking one of the cats, his spear held high as he pierced one of the cat's throats. He was big and he was fast, lunging for a cat as another pounced on him.

He had just lodged his spear in the one in front of her when Athena saw another crouch to pounce.

"Look out!" she screamed, but the cat was already in the air. It landed on Xul and dug its teeth into his skin.

Xul roared and stretched his hand behind him, gripping the thing by the neck.

As he pulled the cat off him, he used his spear to slice another in mid-air as it lunged at him.

From her perch above the ground, Athena watched him move in awe.

He moved with such speed and intent, slicing through the animals as if they were nothing.

It was a clear display that he was trained for combat.

In a matter of seconds, the animals all lay dead around him and Xul rested his spear in the sand to look up at her.

In the dim light, she could hardly see his features and she had no idea what he was thinking.

Now that the threat was no longer there, she needed to figure out how to get down.

Her leg ached as she tried to move it. Still clinging onto the zehmip's thorns, she chanced a glance over the side of the plant's head.

It was at least a 15-story drop. Well, jumping was off the table, even if her leg wasn't injured.

The only other option was to climb down.

The zehmip's stalk was smooth. All she had to do was wrap her arms and legs around it and slide down slowly.

Gingerly moving, she held onto the zehmip's hairs as she lowered herself.

The plant was not moving. Probably because it was preoccupied with digesting its latest meal.

As she reached over the side of its head and her legs hung off, Athena gritted her teeth as her arms gripped into the hairs, trying to support her body weight.

Those people in Mission Impossible made this type of shit look so easy.

Well, it wasn't.

The muscles in her arms protested; her biceps burned from the exertion.

She was already out of breath and she hadn't even reached the stalk yet.

Xul shouted something but she couldn't understand him from so high up.

She couldn't even see him now, as the twin suns had finally retreated and there was no moon.

Heck, she couldn't even see stars.

As her legs dangled, she lowered herself slowly, grabbing onto the hairs and holding on tightly, all the time gritting her teeth and trying to ignore the fire in her arms.

Soon, she was at the bottom of the zehmip's head and she swung her legs to wrap them around the stalk.

That completed, she was finally able to lower herself and grab hold of the stalk with both hands.

As she slid down the stalk and reached the bottom, two big, strong arms enveloped her and pulled her off the zehmip.

Athena made to protest, but she was just too exhausted at that moment to say anything.

She was vaguely aware that he was leading her away from the zehmip.

After a few steps, Xul put her down on the sand and she leaned against him.

He fumbled with something that made a sound and then a light was being held close to her face.

His face was mostly in shadow but she could see concern knitting his brow.

"Why didn't you cry out for help?" He studied her face.

"I was too busy being hauled away by a hell-cat, if you didn't notice."

Xul paused.

"You are troublesome. More so than the rest of your species," he said.

Athena wanted to laugh at that. Apparently, he hadn't heard of Joan of Arc or Helen of Troy.

"I should have found a way to leave you on the ship. It would have been safer for you there," he grunted.

"No," Athena said through gritted teeth. "It would not be safer there. I would rather deal with hell-cats and zehmips in every waking second than return to that ship."

He seemed to consider that for a second before amusement flooded his eyes, and something else...awe?

"They are sand cats," he said. "I have never heard of anyone riding a zehmip before. Your species is more intelligent than I expect, for ones coming from an undeveloped rock."

Oh, this guy. So many compliments.

Balancing on her good leg, Athena tried to yank her arm away from him, but it only caused him to pull her towards his chest. His loincloth brushed against her and she remembered immediately that the darn cat had ripped off the little covering that she had been wearing.

Her naked thighs brushed against his but he didn't seem to take note of that. Instead, he leaned towards her, bringing his face danger-ously close to hers.

She couldn't move. Something about his eyes kept her frozen and she remained rigid, his breath fanning over her cheeks.

"You are peculiar," he said, his eyes narrowing as they searched her face.

"Enough with the compliments," Athena breathed, jerking away from his chest. The action caused her to put too much pressure on the leg that had been bitten and she yelped.

Xul kneeled immediately and grabbed her leg, putting his light source close to inspect the wound.

Muttering something that sounded suspiciously like a curse word, Xul stood and pulled he zehmip coat from his shoulders.

In one smooth movement, he ripped a narrow strip from the coat and kneeled again.

Taking her leg in his hand, he bound the wound tightly, then stood, his eyes focusing on hers.

"We must move," he said. "The scent of blood carries over these sands and there are much more dangerous things here than sand-cats."

Athena raised an eyebrow. "Fine," she said, pulling off her zehmip coat and securing it around her waist. "Just let me make a new skirt."

As soon as she finished, Xul gripped her by the waist and hoisted her over his shoulder.

"Just what do you think you're doing?!" Athena whispered harshly into his back, slamming her fists into the wall his muscles created.

"You cannot be trusted to walk behind me," he said. "I do not need any more zehmip joyrides for tonight."

Athena frowned. "You think I went on that thing for fun! Have you—"

But the slight vibration against her told her he was making fun of her.

Haha.

Very funny.

She'd like to see how he'd fare riding a zehmip.

14

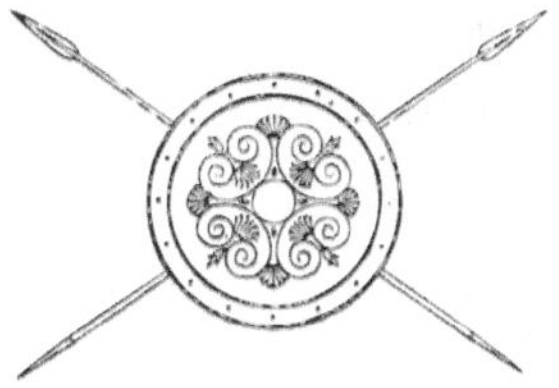

He couldn't tell if she was sleeping or not.

Since the attack of the sand-cats, she had been pretty silent and he had been walking for over three hours now.

He was tempted to ask if she was alright, but he didn't want to risk starting a conversation.

The more he spoke with her, the more he was beginning to like the little human, and that was a problem.

He needed to remain objective. Focused. Eyes on the mission.

He was already crossing boundaries he should not be crossing...but making her flustered gave him such pleasure.

It was strange. She was so helpless, yet she'd managed to defend herself enough to escape the attack of not one, but six sand-cats.

That was impressive in his book. And she hadn't used any weapons, just her plain ingenuity.

It was a story he would tell for many years.

Keeping his focus ahead, he trudged through the sand, his ears perked for any sounds. They still had a long way to go, but at least, when she wasn't walking behind him, he could go at his own pace.

Now, lying over his shoulder, her weight didn't bother him. Years training in the barracks under intense conditions had prepared him for anything Muk had to throw his way.

The only thing he hadn't been prepared for was her.

Athena.

Xul frowned as her name echoed in his mind. It was a strange name but a strong one.

But she was unpredictable and he did not like unpredictable.

Keeping his head straight, he was very aware that her rump was right by his cheek. Even without turning his head he could catch a whiff of her unique female human scent.

It was an intriguing smell.

One that made him forget the mission for a second...one that brought his mind to other things and made him want to turn his head so he could smell her better.

Her soft body seemed to melt against his as he carried her—a constant reminder that he was carrying a woman.

Xul took a deep breath and pushed on, clenching his teeth as another wayward thought crossed his mind.

For many years, he had stayed away from women for this very reason.

They were distracting and he had no time for distractions.

He was so close now.

So close to ending this mission. Something he had dedicated a decade of his life to.

Athena coughed over his shoulder and Xul clenched his teeth harder.

Maybe her presence was a test. He had been so focused on bringing the High Tasqals down that maybe this little human was a reminder of the reason he had set out on this mission in the first place. Maybe she was a reminder that he was doing this to avenge her, Xan, his sister.

A wave of emotion hit him as he thought of his little sister.

She'd been taken when she was only nine orbits old. A day from her tenth orbit day. Taken by an Isclit slave ship and sold to a High Tasqal who had kept her as his pet.

Xul gulped.

Eventually, the High Tasqal had wanted more than entertainment and had used her for his other pleasures, infecting her with its disease.

She had died while trying to bear its young, but even then the disease would have taken her life anyway.

He'd joined the Restitution just for that reason. To avenge Xan. He was going to find every last one of the Tasqals, the scourge of the universe, and rid them of their existence.

Xul let out a blast of hot air from his nose as he remembered finding Xan's body on his first mission into a High Tasqal stronghold.

She had been so little, her enlarged belly had been almost three times her size.

Even thinking about it now, rage filled his entire body.

She was the reason he was doing this.

He would see it to the end.

"Ouch! You're holding me a bit too tight there big guy," Athena murmured, her voice floating up to his ear.

Xul loosened his grip and readjusted her on his shoulder.

"I can walk, you know," she muttered.

"You cannot. Your feet are stripped bare by the sand and your leg has been gnawed."

He felt her body rise and fall on him as she sighed.

"Yea, well, it's not very dignified being carried like this, is it?"

Xul snorted. This was why she was distracting.

"I don't care about your dignity," he said.

Athena huffed. "Of all the aliens, I just had to be stuck with the one who's Mr. Cynical." She paused, then murmured almost inaudibly, "I guess it could be worse."

Xul snorted again and felt as she pressed against his back with her small hand to raise her head.

"It's pitch black out here," she whispered. "How do you even know where you're going?"

"I have a navigator."

She let out another huff, a sound that was so incredibly human.

He hadn't heard anyone do it before but since being around her it was something he'd heard so many times now.

"I know you have that thing but how do you know where you are going. I can't see a thing," she said, raising her body a little higher.

"I can see through the darkness. Not as well as when the suns are traversing the sky but well enough."

"You mean you have night vision?" He could sense she was looking back at him now. "Well, I'll be damned. I can't see shit. Why are you aliens so gifted yet we humans have...what do we have anyway?"

Xul let out a chuckle. "So you admit your species is frail and unsuited to the universe," he said.

"I do not! I only mean that you all just...you've evolved like wild animals. Maybe we humans spent more time developing our brains."

Xul snorted again. If she was saying her species was intelligent, he'd let her have that. Either intelligent or incredibly stupid. Her stunt with the zehmip is yet to be categorized under one of those things.

"Can't you walk with a torch or something? What if one of those cats is around?"

"A torch will only bring attention to us. If any ships are patrolling overhead, they would see us easily," he replied.

"I thought you said no one will come looking for us." He could feel her small frame tense against him.

She was right to be concerned. It was something he did not want to deal with either.

"Your species is precious cargo. Small. Easily transportable. And far away from your home planet."

A grunt escaped her.

"Nice to know I am precious cargo," she muttered. "A guy had told me that once. Needless to say, we didn't work out."

Xul's body shook as he chuckled before sobering and pressing onward.

Another reason why she was a distraction.

He quite enjoyed her little human quips.

"How much longer till daylight?" she asked.

Xul stopped walking and lifted his head. He had picked up a scent before but now it was getting stronger.

"Alien?" she whispered harshly, probably realizing that he'd stopped walking.

"It will rain in a few moments," Xul said.

"So you can smell the rain, too?" she asked.

"You cannot?" Xul glanced over his shoulder. In the darkness, her blue eyes looked like silver and she narrowed them at him.

He couldn't help it; a small smile curved his lips.

Resting her on the sand beneath him, Xul stripped off his zehmip coat.

"You will need this to protect against the rain," he said, handing the coat to her.

He was surprised she didn't argue and just took the coat from him.

Just as she managed to fix it over her upper body, a slew of water rained down on them.

"Goddamn! I thought you meant it was going to rain soon!" she shouted through the downpour. "Not right at this moment!"

Without answering her immediately, Xul hoisted her over his shoulder again.

"Muk is unpredictable," he said, as he trudged through the troughs that were already forming beneath his feet.

With the added wetness, the sand became even more dangerous, forming quicksand in some places. It was even more reason for him to carry her. He could spot the areas of danger. She could not. She couldn't even see far in the darkness.

The rain was beating down on them hard, making it impossible for them to talk.

It was probably for the best, Xul thought.

Talking to her made him come to that dangerous tipping point of enjoying her company...and that would only lead to disaster in the future.

15

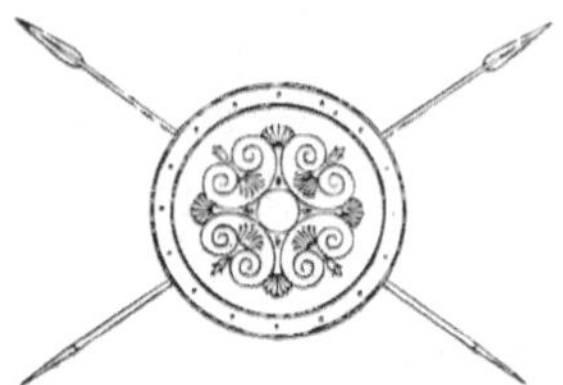

For the next two hours, the rain beat down on them, and the temperature had dropped the moment it began.

Never-ending sand. Man-eating plants. Hell-cats. And now torrential rain.

She wasn't sure Planet Muk had any redeeming qualities.

Beneath her, Xul was steady and sure. He was pushing through the rain as if it wasn't coming down like a monsoon.

The water seemed to slide off his suede-like skin easily and she reckoned that was because of the soft fuzz that covered his body. He could stand in the rain and he wouldn't get soaked.

She, on the other hand, was shivering from the cold even under the zehmip coat.

Xul's warm skin against hers was the only thing keeping her temperature stable and without intending to, she snuggled further into him.

He didn't seem to mind, or he didn't notice.

As the suns slowly rose, a dim orange glow covered the landscape, and though the rain continued, it didn't fall as hard as when it began.

Xul stopped again and she assumed he was checking his little gadget with the dials.

He'd been stopping every few minutes to do just that, she assumed, to ensure that he wasn't straying from his course.

Athena sighed against him, another shiver going through her body.

He felt good. Warm. Masculine.

Those weren't thoughts she'd been expecting to feel, especially not after waking up in a cell with him as one of her captors.

She heard him grunt as he trudged on through the wet sand.

It was as if he had no lapse in his stamina.

He just kept on going, and going, and going like Excedrin. He just kept pushing forward. Either he had unending energy or he was pushed forward with a greater purpose in mind.

She assumed it was the latter, and after what he'd told her about the High Tasqals, she understood why.

To think that she would have ended up as a sex slave to one of those beasts made her forget about the rain and the fact that it was so cold. If it hadn't been for Xul, even though he hadn't intended it, she would have been stuck on that ship.

For the second time, her mind ran on the human women who were still stranded there and her heart clenched.

They were her only link back to Earth, but it wasn't only about that.

She needed to help them escape.

She'd have wanted them to do the same for her.

THE RAIN HAD NOW SLOWED to a trickle and the suns were a little higher in the sky.

Xul stopped walking suddenly and eased her off his shoulder.

She was still shivering as he rested her onto the sand, a frown on his face as he looked down at her.

Through a shiver, Athena met his gaze and knew exactly what he was thinking.

"Look, no more compliments from you right now, ok? I know I am ill-suited to this environment."

"I was not going to compliment you," he said.

Despite the fact that it felt like she was freezing, Athena managed to roll her eyes at him. "I was being sarcastic."

She noticed a small smile curve the corner of his lips and she looked away.

She shouldn't be thinking about the way he looked right now.

The fact that when he smiled he looked handsome shouldn't be on her mind.

Especially not now. And not ever.

He was a bull-man.

Athena gulped and pulled the zehmip cloak closer around her.

"We rest here today," Xul said, turning away.

Not far from them was a sleeping zehmip underneath a dune.

Athena watched as Xul trudged through the wet sand towards the plant.

All around them, the water from the rain created shallow pools and she wondered if it was safe to drink.

Probably not.

She'd already lucked out with the atmosphere being breathable. She wasn't going to push her luck with the water being drinkable. So far, Muk had taught her that nothing was what it seemed.

Her body still trembling, her attention was drawn to the sound of bark stretching as Xul woke up the zehmip.

With as much skill as she had seen him use the day before, he provoked the plant and cut it down.

Soon, he was hauling the long head and stalk behind him as he headed back her way.

Something close by in the sand glistened in the light and caught Athena's attention.

Crawling over to it, she realized it was a piece of metal that had been uncovered by the rainwater washing the sand away.

Pulling at it, she managed to dislodge it from the sand.

It was triangular and sharp around the edges. It looked like a piece of a spaceship that had crashed on the planet a long time ago.

Digging around the area, she found no other pieces.

Never mind, she was sure she could find perfect use for the piece that she found.

As Xul reached her and began cutting the zehmip and setting up the tent, he eyed the piece of metal but said nothing—not that him objecting to her carrying it was going to make her leave it anyway.

As he set up the tent, Xul also stripped the hairy skin off the zehmip and laid it over the wet sand inside the tent.

He was already cutting up the zehmip stalk when Athena crawled over to him, biting back the pain she was feeling in her leg.

She hoped to God it wasn't infected.

Grabbing one of the stalks, she watched what Xul was doing and mimicked his actions, pushing the pointed edge of the metal shrapnel into the stalk to cut a straight line.

Xul raised an eyebrow as he watched her but he continued working without saying anything.

As the stalk split, he then bent it from the edges, forcing the center to pucker before driving his blade inside to remove the remainder of the skin.

Athena followed and did the same thing.

She noticed he stuck the hard part in the sand to make a part of the barrier and the other part he put down for later.

Athena assumed it had the thick yellow meat inside.

Doing a few more, she was happy with the piece of metal.

It would make the perfect weapon, for now.

As Xul pulled the last few pieces of the stalk into the tent, she followed in behind him.

He was busy husking the other bit when she entered and closed the barrier behind her.

Resting on the ground behind him, she watched him work for a few seconds.

He was quiet and she wondered what he was thinking about.

Pulling her injured leg toward her, she winced at the pain the movement caused.

Gritting her teeth, she unwrapped the bandage to see a nasty wound where the sand-cat had bitten her. Inhaling deeply, she secured the bandage. She'd have to get it looked at as soon as she could but there was nothing she could do about it now.

It seemed Xul finished husking the zehmip's flesh because he rested his spear to the side and fell back onto his back, gazing at her from his position.

"You are still shivering," he said.

Athena looked down at her arms. She hadn't noticed.

"It will stop as soon as I get warm. I just need to get out of these wet clothes..." Athena trailed off.

She didn't have anything to change into and she wasn't going to walk around naked.

"Do what you must," Xul said, still watching her. "Or you will catch a desert cold."

Athena nodded. She assumed that was just like a regular cold, just made more annoying by the fact that they were stranded in the desert.

Opening the barrier, she limped out of the tent. The little warmth of the sun was comforting but it wasn't enough.

The temperature drop from the rain made it still too cold. Xul was right. She needed to find a way to warm herself soon or she would get sick and she definitely didn't need to give him another reason to point out just how unsuited she was for life anywhere outside of Earth.

She would need to strip off the coats and let them dry. She'd be naked but he'd seen her naked before and he hadn't seemed to notice.

Maybe men of his kind were different.

Or maybe he was gay.

Didn't matter.

She needed to get out of the clothes and she also needed to urinate. Badly.

Glancing around, the ground dipped a little way off. She could stoop down there and relieve herself away from the tent.

Gripping the little metal shrapnel in her hand, she limped off toward the dip in the sand.

Her feet sunk about an inch with every step she took and she could feel the moisture between her toes.

Turning to glance back at the tent, she was satisfied with the distance. At least she could pee in private.

Stooping, her view of the tent disappeared over the mound of sand.

Sighing, Athena waited for her bladder to empty.

Once again, her mind ran on the other women back on the ship.

She needed to do better.

Right now she was too dependent on Xul. If she was going to meet up with them and return to Earth, she needed to figure out a way to beat the odds that were against her.

As she finished up peeing, her body still shivering in the cold, a sound behind her made her turn sharply.

There was nothing there.

Athena squinted and gripped on to the metal shrapnel, her ears perked and her eyes alert.

She was sure she'd heard something.

Standing on her shaky legs, she tried not to put any pressure on the wound as she backed away from the area slowly.

As she moved away, she saw the sand move around her and her eyes widened.

Fuck. She wasn't alone. And whatever it was, it was big.

Gripping the shrapnel in her hand, she walked backward, her feet sinking as she stepped.

Maybe she could get away before whatever it was that she'd disturbed came awake.

But she wasn't to be in such luck.

As the sand shuddered around her, Athena lost her balance and fell on her already injured leg.

Pain shot up through her bone but there was no time to pay attention to it as something long and scaly rose from the sand.

Light glistened off the scales and Athena blinked as she scuttled backward.

She could see right through the thing.

It was frickin' transparent. No wonder she hadn't seen it at first.

But as its body rose, the scales seemed to flip over and turn from transparent to a shiny black.

A scream lodged in her throat.

The thing looked like a giant anaconda only its head looked like that of a thorny dragon.

What the actual fuck!

The thing dived for her and Athena managed to roll out of the way, causing it to smash its face into the sand.

For a second it went transparent, then the scales flipped again and it lunged at her.

Athena rolled again and the thing's head crashed into the sand right beside her.

It was clear it wasn't just going to let her go.

To be honest, she wouldn't have taken kindly to it visiting her house to take a piss either.

It would either kill her or she it. She preferred the latter.

As it lunged for her again, Athena rolled, but it caught a piece of the zehmip cloak and pulled her up high into the air.

As she swung helplessly in the air, she gripped the piece of metal shrapnel and aimed for the thing's neck.

Driving the metal with all her strength, she lodged it in the thing's scales and it let her go, releasing a loud hiss.

She was hanging on only by the metal now and it was cutting into her hand but it was either that or falling to the sand and breaking something.

Damn. She wished she'd known she was going to be abducted.

A gym membership would have been taken out a month prior to this.

Swinging her legs, she wrapped them around the thing's neck as it thrashed about. Pulling out the metal shrapnel, she drove it deep again.

A scream left her lips as she drove the shrapnel again and again and again. And then, just as the thing began falling to the ground, something hit her hard in the head.

Her vision faded for a second, but not before she saw another of the creatures right behind her. It had tried to bite her and had missed, but not before its big head collided with her, its hard skull connecting with hers.

As she and the animal she'd stabbed fell, she saw the other lunging for her.

She needed to fight.

She couldn't pass out right now.

But her body wasn't listening.

All she felt was cold.

As her body hit the sand, darkness enveloped her vision.

She was cold.

So, so cold.

16

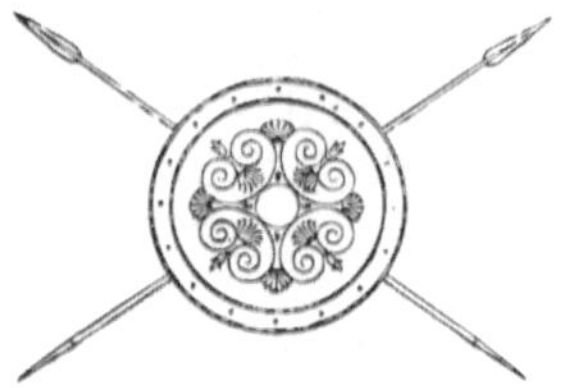

Xul heard the scream and his head popped up from the floor.

Qrak.

Not again.

Dashing out of the tent, his eyes widened at the scene a little ways off from him.

Two uloms were attacking the little human.

"Qrak!" he said underneath his breath as he sprinted toward her, spear in hand.

She was stabbing one of the uloms with the little piece of metal she had found but she had not yet seen the other. Uloms traveled in twos. They always did.

Qrak. It was a wonder she managed to find so much trouble.

He'd thought she was just outside the tent trying to get herself warm under the rising suns.

Instead, she'd managed to wander into the uloms' den.

She was fighting for her life and Xul's heart beat hard as he came upon them.

She better not die.

He swallowed hard as he lunged for the second ulom.

She better not die!

Something inside him was terrified of that happening but he had no time to evaluate where that feeling was coming from.

As he drove his spear into the second ulom, the thing swung its head toward Athena and, thankfully, its bite missed. But its skull connected with hers and Xul watched in horror as she almost lost her balance off the ulom she was fighting.

Driving his spear again, the second ulom reared in pain.

As he watched the ulom Athena was attached to fall, he sliced the second ulom straight up its midsection.

Thick yellow blood squirted all over the sand and Xul dropped his spear and he rushed toward Athena.

She wasn't moving.

The little human wasn't moving.

Xul's heart beat hard as he finally reached her and pulled her into his arms.

She was still gripping on to the metal object, even though her hands were bleeding from the metal sinking into her skin.

Bending his head to her chest, he sensed the slight flutter of her heart.

She was still alive.

Unconscious, but alive.

Xul leaned his head back and stared up into the light orange sky.

She was going to be the death of him.

A low chuckle rumbled in his chest from both relief and disbelief.

How did one so unassuming invite so much trouble?

Pulling her into his arms, he picked up his spear and brought her back to the tent, where he rested her softly against the zehmip skin on the floor.

Her skin was like ice and the twin suns hadn't risen enough yet to provide enough warmth.

Xul cursed underneath his breath again as he weighed his options.

If he didn't do something, she was going to get ill.

Stripping off the wet zehmip coats she'd wrapped around herself, he set them outside the tent for them to dry.

She was naked and shivering in front of him now.

On her head, the gash that had been there after the crash landing was now bleeding again after the impact with the ulom.

Her leg was bleeding and so were her hands.

He needed to do something fast.

Cutting strips from the zehmip skin on the floor, he wrapped them tightly around her wounds to put pressure on them.

As soon as she regained consciousness, he would have to go search for more desert flowers to help heal her wounds. He didn't know how long it took humans to heal but he guessed the healing process was slow.

As she shivered on the ground beside him, she looked so small, soft...and female.

But he shouldn't be thinking about that. That was the last thing that should be in his mind.

His priority right now was keeping her alive.

Keeping her alive and getting to that outpost on time.

Glancing toward the exit, he contemplated leaving her to go search for another zehmip so he could make use of the skin to keep her warm. But the last dune he'd seen had been a way off.

If he left her in this state, he wouldn't forgive himself if something happened.

Not that she meant that much to him...did she?

Was she beginning to mean something to him?

He brushed the thought aside.

He'd keep her warm then.

Lying on the zehmip skin beside her, he pulled her body into his and wrapped himself around her. His body heat would warm her up and ward off the cold.

He was only doing it to save her life.

Xul gulped as her body settled against his.

Qrak. She was so soft. A distinct softness against his hardness.

It had been many moons since he had felt the softness of a woman against him.

Not that he hadn't had offers, but he had only indulged when he had needed the release.

This somehow felt...different.

This wasn't about relieving pent up stress.

This was about comfort.

Xul shook his head.

It was not about comfort.

It was about saving her life. Plain and simple.

Nothing else.

Dipping his chin to her head, he inhaled her scent. She was dirty, but underneath that, he could smell her unique female essence. It was...inviting and he felt himself harden.

Dammit.

He needed to get whatever feelings were developing under control.

This mission was too important to get sidetracked.

ATHENA'S EYES fluttered open and for a second, she thought that she was back in her bed in her apartment.

But as her eyes opened some more, she realized she was still in hell.

Why did hell feel so good all of a sudden? Not hot, but warm, comforting...and hard.

Her eyes opened fully then.

Hell was only warm because someone big and heavy had their body draped over hers. And that hard thing...well, somebody was a little excited.

Athena gulped but didn't move.

Her head was resting on his arm and she wondered if he was sleeping.

The last thing she remembered was falling off that invisible snake-dragon thing and seeing the other one lunge at her.

He must have saved her...again.

Her head ached and so did her hand and her leg. Damn, she was really fucked up.

Roughly two days into this and she was already half-dead.

Well, at least she wasn't shivering anymore.

Glancing down at herself without moving her head, Athena's eyelids fluttered and she resisted a groan.

She was naked.

Her cheeks flushed, and as if it was listening to her inner thoughts, she felt the hardness behind her pulse.

Shit.

Her breathing came a little more ragged but she did not move.

For some reason, she didn't want to.

Not yet.

For the first time in this horrible journey, she felt...comfortable.

She couldn't see his face, but judging from his breathing, he was sleeping.

Athena settled back against him, as she tried to ignore the hardness poking into her back.

Xul felt good. Bull-man or not, he felt damn good and a soft sigh escaped her lips.

It had been a while since she had cuddled with anyone. Trust her to have to travel across the galaxy just to find something to cuddle with. Working a nine-to-five job at the pharmacy hadn't really given her many options, though. It was either hook up with some random guy after work or hop on a dating website and try to find something more meaningful.

She'd tried both.

Results: not good.

Turning slightly, she twisted so she was on her back and could see Xul's face.

His eyes were closed but his arm was still draped around her.

Dropping her eyes to his loincloth, Athena held back another gasp.

He was packing. Definitely packing. That bulge told a helluva lot.

When her eyes refocused on his face, her gaze met green ones and she flushed immediately.

He wasn't sleeping at all.

"How do you feel?" he asked softly. His face was close. So, so close.

Athena swallowed hard. "Better." She blinked. "Thank you for saving me."

A small smile smoothed his lips. "I didn't save you. I helped you out. You managed to take out one of the uloms on your own."

"I did?" Athena raised an eyebrow.

"Yes," Xul said, his voice still low and the way he said it made her think he found that impressive.

"Oh," she breathed, running her tongue over her bottom lip. Xul's gaze fell on that movement and his eyes stayed there.

"I'm naked," Athena whispered.

"Yes," he said, his gaze rising slowly back to her eyes.

They lay gazing at each other for the next few moments and Athena didn't want to break the moment.

There was something intense about his eyes, something that drew her in and made her feel like nothing else outside the tent mattered.

Her hand touched his cheek before she even realized what she was doing. The action surprised them both, but apart from a slight jerk, Xul didn't pull away.

Athena swallowed hard again before moving her fingers up toward his brow to run them over the ridges that led to his horns.

There was something frickin' sensual about it and it was making her heart beat hard, but she didn't stop.

Xul was watching her intently as her fingers moved but neither of them said anything.

She hadn't noticed them before, but she could feel some small hard bumps dotting the length of his eyebrow.

As she ran her fingers over them and over the ridges of his horn, she brought her index finger down the length of his nose and ran it around the ring that was there.

The metal looked like gold and as she traced her finger around it Xul raised his hand and brushed her hair behind her ears.

Athena shivered at the feel of his touch and Xul frowned slightly.

"Still cold?"

"No, I—" Athena blinked a few times to clear her thoughts. Just what was she doing?

This was wrong, wasn't it?

But when she raised her eyes to his and her gaze fell to his lips, a sudden intense feeling rushed over her. What was so wrong about it?

She had no answer.

Raising her head slowly, Athena swallowed hard, her gaze focused on his lips as she drew near to them. She felt Xul stiffen beside her but he didn't move away.

As their lips touched, what she could only describe as a lightning bolt ran through her spine and she wondered if he felt it too.

His lips were firm against hers and as she ran her tongue over his bottom lip, Xul let out a groan and turned to pin her beneath him.

His tongue forced her mouth open and then he was kissing her.

Athena gasped into his mouth.

His kiss was fierce and butterflies fluttered underneath her eyelids as she opened her mouth to his. He tasted good. So good. So unexpectedly good and she found herself returning his kiss with as much fervor as he was giving her. His tongue was larger than hers and thicker and the way it curved around hers had her moaning underneath him.

As the sound reached his ears, Xul paused to look down at her, his eyes searching hers.

"Why'd you stop?" she croaked. God, that was not something she thought she'd be asking him.

There was conflict in his eyes and he blinked a few times as if trying to sort through his thoughts.

"I should get you a fresh coat and desert flowers to heal your wounds," he said, his voice hoarse.

She couldn't hide the disappointment that suddenly flooded her features and Athena just nodded.

Xul gulped as he eased himself off her and grabbed his spear.

"Do not leave the tent," he said.

Athena nodded, pulling her legs toward herself.

Her nakedness made her feel open and vulnerable and those feelings couldn't be stronger at this moment.

Grabbing his spear, Xul gave her one final glance before exiting the tent.

He was gone for what felt like hours but she was sure it wasn't that long.

In the meantime, Athena had checked her wounds, and he was right. She needed some healing or at least some better bandages.

The zehmip skin he'd put outside the tent was now dry and she'd pulled them inside to try and turn them into something more fit for travel.

Cutting small strips to use as thread, she used the metal shrapnel to hack the zehmip coat into a pair of trousers and closed the legs with the thread. She also made a drawstring waist.

Now for the blouse, she had to settle on a poncho type of covering and a wide band to tie her breasts back.

Putting the ensemble on, she was sure she wouldn't make it to Paris Fashion Week but it would have to do.

The remaining scraps of zehmip skin she used to wrap around a section of the metal shrapnel that she held in her hand. That way, she wouldn't get cut again.

She'd just decided to lie down again when she heard movement outside the tent.

The suns were still high in the sky so she assumed it was just after midday so no creatures should be messing about, right?

Her mind ran on the invisible snake-dragon thing. Maybe not all creatures.

Grabbing the piece of metal shrapnel, she crouched with it in her hand as the barrier opened and Xul popped his head in, his face coming inches away from the metal edge.

He glanced at the thing, then at her, and she could see a small smile grace his features.

Athena gulped and lowered her weapon before scooting to the side.

She eyed him as he entered the tent and put down the zehmip skin he'd fetched. He also had some kind of long rope that looked like he'd made it out of twine.

When he glanced at her again, it seemed he finally noticed she was clothed.

"You've been busy," he said, crouching before her.

Athena didn't answer.

Was he just going to not talk about what happened earlier?

Well, she could play that game too.

In his hand, he produced the same flowers she'd seen him use on her earlier and he motioned to her that she should give him her leg.

The limb pained as she stretched it out to him and Xul unwrapped the bandage.

Crushing the petals in his hand, he cut a strip of zehmip skin, placed the crushed petals within it, and rewrapped her leg.

He did the same thing to her arm and head.

When he was finished, he turned his back to her and began husking the zehmip stalk.

As she watched him work, what she could only describe as a feeling of rejection hit her like a brick.

Had she done something wrong?

Said something?

Did she smell?

He'd kissed her back. Didn't that mean he'd wanted to?

Trying to ignore the questions in her mind, she watched him work for a few more seconds before she moved the barrier to gaze out into the desert.

It was so unassuming, the sand out there. One wouldn't guess the dangers that were hiding out there, some in plain sight.

Something glistened in the distance and Athena squinted.

She was sure she had seen something in the light. But there was nothing. She was about to move her gaze from the spot when she saw something reflect in the light again and her eyes widened.

"Xul," she whispered, craning her neck a little further. She did see something and it was flying in the distance. It looked like a spaceship. It had to be a spaceship.

"Xul," she said, a little louder. "Are there inhabitants on this planet?"

She heard him pause what he was doing and assumed he was now looking her way.

"Muk is largely undeveloped and the Mukkians are few. But yes," he said.

"So, they wouldn't have spaceships, would they?"

In a second, he was beside her.

"Qrak," he said underneath his breath. Grabbing his spear and the fresh rope he'd made, he glanced back out the barrier.

It was still far away but they could see it better now and it was definitely a spaceship.

"Is that..." Athena's eyes widened. "That's not your friends, is it?"

A look at Xul answered her question.

His eyes had gone hard and his jaw was ticking.

"We must move," he said, "before they spot us."

He didn't even wait. She was just able to grab her metal shrapnel before he was pulling her out of the tent by her good arm. As soon as they were out, he collapsed the tent and began heaping sand over it.

Taking the cue, Athena helped him cover the tent and soon he was pulling her by the hand again.

"The food..." she murmured.

"We will have to hunt again later."

We.

Athena blinked. She'd have to dissect that thought later.

There was a dip in the sand and Xul was pulling her down it. Athena grit her teeth against the pain that was shooting up her leg and ignored it. Her heart was hammering in her chest.

There was only one reason why Xul would be acting like this.

Their captors were after them.

As they ran down the dune, Athena lost her footing and fell on her side, causing Xul to lose his balance as well. There was no way to stop what happened next, and they both slid down the hill of sand to the bottom.

The sand was coarse and grated on her skin. She was sure she was going to have some horrible friction burns later.

As they reached the bottom, Xul was up on his feet in a second, his eyes wild as he glanced around them. Then it looked like he spotted something and, holding her hand, he pulled her toward it.

It was a hole in the side of a dune and she heard him mutter something that sounded like a curse as he stepped in it.

It was big enough for him to crouch in and Athena just had to bend her head.

Xul had his spear poised for battle and Athena gripped the metal for reassurance, ready for a fight if they had to. They were ducked into the dark space when she turned her wide eyes on Xul. He was looking at her with his finger on his lips.

Got it.

Be quiet.

Athena almost held her breath as they waited, her ears perked for any sound.

Around them, she noticed the same flowers he'd been using to put on her wounds were growing out of the sand.

She'd have to get some before they left.

The sound of the spacecraft was close now, almost like it was hovering directly above them.

She squeezed the hand that was holding hers and Xul met her gaze.

Maybe they would fly over them and continue searching some-place else.

Please let them fly over and go search—

But then it hit her and Athena inhaled so deeply that her back arched against the walls of the cave.

She knew this pain.

She remembered it.

They'd found them.

17

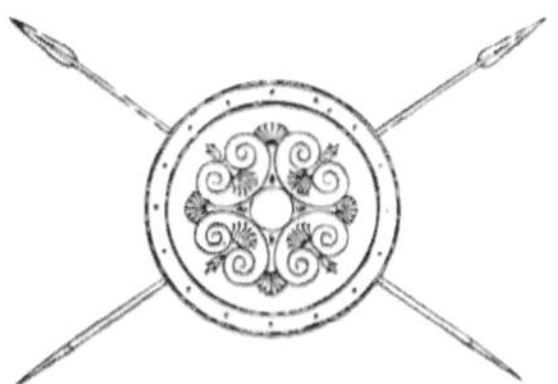

Her entire body trembled though there was nothing in her immediate location that was causing the pain. And whoever it was that was holding on to the torture remote wasn't stopping.

She couldn't breathe as the fire in her veins threatened to eat her up.

She was going to die.

She was going to die if they didn't stop it.

In the midst of the pain, the thought crossed her mind that death was probably their intention.

They meant to kill her if she did not show herself.

Athena's fingers dug into the sand beneath her as her entire body twisted and writhed. She was breaking apart from the inside out.

Her vision went in and out and in those flashes, she saw Xul's murderous expression as he crouched over her.

He was about to dash outside of their hiding place when she gripped his hand, tears running down her cheeks as she tried to speak through the pain, her body convulsing as it pulsed through her entire frame.

They'd never pressed the button for this long before.

They were trying to kill her.

But if Xul went out, they would kill him too.

She couldn't allow that.

His mission depended on him getting back into space. He needed to get to the outpost.

If they didn't find him, then there was a chance the other women still stranded on the ship had a chance to escape back to Earth.

Xul seemed to read her eyes and his expression became even more murderous. Pulling out of her grasp, he dashed out of the hiding spot and into the light.

THE LIGHT OUTSIDE was blinding for a second but Xul didn't care. They were killing her. He didn't think she understood what they had done to her while she was unconscious but it was evident the biological microorganisms they'd pumped into her body were still functional, and the Isclits were emitting that signal that made the little organisms destroy their host from the inside out.

As he looked above, the wind generated from the ship's engine blew sand across him.

He could see their faces.

An Isclit and two of their guards.

Aiming his spear, he could see them snarl at him as he tried to get the trajectory right in his head. He knew where the engine was on the ship. He just had to pierce it and the thing would fall.

He just had to—

The first shot hit him in the side and made him stagger. Gripping the area, he pulled his hand away and it was covered in blood.

He looked up just in time to see them aim at him again, but he managed to dive out of the way, falling to his knees as blood rose in his throat.

They shot again, and this time it caught him in the leg.

Xul roared in pain, as his vision turned red.

He was not going down like this.

Ten years would not end like this.

Grabbing his spear, he pulled back and aimed, throwing the spear through the air with all his strength.

He heard as it pierced through the metal and a stray shot whizzed by his head.

As the ship teetered, one of the gator-guards jumped out and ran towards him.

His entire body was in pain, the wounds were deep, but he was not going to die here.

Today was not his day.

A growl from somewhere behind him in the cave made his heart almost stop.

Athena.

She was not safe.

He knew it hadn't been wise to enter the sandcats' den but it had been their only choice. The sound of the ship must have woken the beasts.

As he coughed up more blood, his vision going in and out, he staggered to his feet and tried to head back in her direction.

He could not let her come to harm.

He didn't know how he felt about her yet but he'd felt one thing strongly after they'd kissed.

That feeling of possessiveness.

A need to make her his.

It was something he'd been able to fight when they weren't in danger, but now, now it was coursing through his veins.

"Athena!" he called out. "Run!"

He was just able to see her crawling from the hiding spot when the gator-guard pounced on him from behind and he crashed into the sand.

The thing was strong, gripping his throat as it sunk its teeth into his shoulder.

Xul roared as the pain shot through his arm. Rising on his knees, he gripped the guard between the jaws and forced its mouth apart, freeing himself.

As he continued to stretch the thing's mouth to the point of ripping the jaws apart, the gator-guard swung its tail, hitting him in the midsection.

He was mildly aware of something brown dashing towards them and was just able to turn, swinging the gator-guard's body with him and causing the sand-cat that had bounded toward them to bury its sharp teeth into the guard's back.

As the guard released him, Xul saw another small animal running toward the fallen ship.

Athena.

But he had no time to call out to her as he was hit in the head from behind. The other gator-guard had exited the ship and was now digging its sharp claws into his head.

Grasping behind him, Xul grabbed the arms of the guard and launched him over his head. As the guard fell into the sand, a yelp behind him made him turn just in time to see the other gator-guard break the neck of the sand-cat. The guard turned to him now and Xul heard a shout to his right.

Turning, he saw Athena running towards him. Her face was covered with blood and the sight alone made his heart wring in his chest.

She was carrying his spear, the ooze of the Isclit dripping from it, and she headed for the guard that had fallen.

Xul nodded.

Dashing for the one in front, he crashed into him headfirst and the guard roared, its head lolling backward.

The exertion made his vision blur and Xul could feel his own blood running from his wounds and coating his body.

He needed to get rid of them.

He needed to at least make sure she was safe, if it was the last thing he did.

He could feel the gator-guard's blood against his face as his horn impaled the beast. It screamed and thrashed around him, digging its claws deep into his skin as it died.

One more.

He just needed to take out one more and then she would be safe.

Turning, Xul's vision darkened and he could hear his heart beating in his ears.

Just one more.

He staggered forward, only to fall on his knees.

He was losing too much blood. He could hardly see.

But he needed to protect her.

He needed to.

In the dimness of his vision, he saw a little body dashing forward, a war cry echoing from her lips as she drove his spear deep into the second gator-guard, just sliding low enough in the sand for its tail to miss her.

The guard cried out and clutched at the spear in its chest but the little fighter hung on, pushing it as deep as she could.

Its tail swung again, but this time she wasn't so lucky.

It hit her head on and she was knocked away into the sand.

Athena...

Xul choked on the blood in his mouth.

Must save...Athena.

Got to save...

Athena.

His vision darkened as her name died on his lips.

18

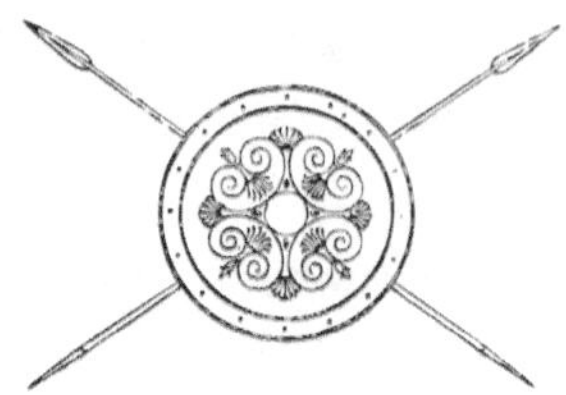

Athena regained consciousness with a start.

The suns were going down and every bone in her body hurt.

Her wounds were bleeding afresh and dried blood was caked over her face.

Her body trembled as she rose, pain shooting through her frame.

Xul.

She could see him. He was lying face down in the sand.

Her stomach clenched.

Crawling on her hands and knees, she crawled past the gator-guard with Xul's spear still jutting from its chest. The other guard lay crumpled not far from Xul.

"Xul," she whispered when she reached him.

He wasn't moving and tears were already forming in her eyes.

No. He couldn't die.

Not now.

"Xul!" With the little strength that she had, she turned him over and her heart caught in her throat.

There was blood everywhere. Coating his body and coating the sand beneath him.

Oh God.

This was all because of her.

He'd have never exited the hiding spot if it hadn't been for her.

Checking for his pulse, she tried to calm her nerves.

There was something there, but it was faint.

Very faint.

Another sob caught in her throat as she looked about them.

There was nothing but carnage, death, and wilderness.

Glancing back at the ship that had crashed, she realized that it must have blown up while she was unconscious.

Didn't matter. She'd already managed to kill the Isclit. Hopefully, before he had radioed for backup.

Now, her main priority was Xul.

He must live.

He had to.

Pulling on the little strength that she had, she limped back to the entrance of the cave and picked as many of the healing flowers as she could. The sand-cat she'd killed was still at the entrance and she kicked the body as she passed.

She knew now why Xul had told her to be quiet. It was a sand-cat den.

This was where he'd risked coming all those times she needed the flowers for her wounds.

Her heart lurched again with gratitude.

Grabbing the rope he'd left behind, she limped over to the gator-guard and pulled the spear from its chest. It made a disgusting wet sound as it exited and her stomach responded by trying to exert its contents. Which consisted of nothing.

She had nothing in there because they hadn't had time to eat.

Looking around them, she eyed a piece of the ship that had blown off. It was probably big enough to put Xul on but she was sure she wouldn't be able to pull the weight of them both.

Glancing up at the sky, Athena set her mouth into a tight line.

She needed to move and she needed to move fast. Night was coming soon and they had no shelter.

Setting her mouth in a tight line, she ignored her body's protests and limped over to Xul, collapsing at his side when she got there.

She needed to survive this.

It was the only way for them to make it out alive. But first, she needed to move him.

Wrapping the rope across his shoulders, she attached the other ends around her own shoulders, tying it tightly.

She knew moving injured people was a bad thing but letting him stay put meant certain death.

As she tried to walk forward, the strain on her shoulders was too much and Xul hardly moved.

Glancing behind her, she gritted her teeth. She'd just have to try harder.

Falling on her knees, she dug her hands into the sand as she pulled her body forward, crying out with the exertion.

It was almost too much, but he moved a little.

That was all she needed to know.

She was going to do it.

She didn't have a choice.

As she crawled forward, Athena forgot the pain and focused ahead.

It was painful and it was slow but she was going to do it.

She wasn't going to give up.

It didn't matter that tears were running down her cheeks or that her bones felt like they were going to break.

She was going to make it back to where they'd camped and she was going to make sure that he was okay.

She was going to make it.

***

NIGHT WAS ALMOST upon them when Athena collapsed. She'd almost made it. Just a few more paces to go.

She could see the area where they'd been camping before. It wasn't far ahead.

Glancing behind her, she gulped hard as she looked at Xul.

He hadn't regained consciousness and she didn't have the heart to check if he was still breathing.

She refused to let those thoughts get in her head.

He wasn't going to die. Not on her watch.

Digging her hands into the sand, she pulled herself forward, inching closer and closer to their abandoned camp, and when she finally reached it, she collapsed and pulled in a ragged breath.

But there was only a little light left in the sky; she didn't have time to take a breather. Unfastening the ropes from around her shoulders, she winced at the pain it caused. Her skin had been rubbed off by the friction and she hadn't even realized.

As she searched underneath the soft sand for the zehmip head, she finally caught one of the thorns and pulled it upward.

It took her a few minutes to set up the tent again. Pushing the thorns as deep in the sand as she could.

Underneath, the zehmip skin that had been there before was still intact. Gripping the rope, she pulled Xul's body into the tent and secured the barriers, breathing hard as she collapsed to take a breath.

He was still not moving and Athena found herself trembling as she leaned over him.

"Xul," she breathed, her body trembling with the effort.

Pulling out the flowers she'd stashed in her bosom, she began crushing the petals together in her palm.

She could hardly see, but she wasn't going to dare search for the light. His satchel must be somewhere under the sand anyway and she wasn't about to go outside the tent looking for it.

Her plan was to remain low and keep quiet till morning.

Hopefully, the predators around would be more attracted to the bodies of the gator-guards still at the scene and Xul would be safe for the night.

As the flowers turned into a pulp, Athena plastered as much as she could over his wounds.

There was a deep hole in his stomach where some sort of laser had shot him and he was bleeding from his head, his back, his legs....fuck.

She tried to get the flower sap into as much of the wounds as she could but it wasn't enough.

For a second, she contemplated making the trek back to the sand-cats' den but decided against it almost immediately.

That would be stupid.

She would only be putting them both in danger.

She would just have to keep put.

Even in the darkness, she could feel the sand that had embedded itself in Xul's wounds and she knew that wasn't good.

She was going to have to find a way to clean his wounds or he was at risk of infection or worse.

She needed water.

And soon.

Shuddering as she lay beside him, she rested her head on his chest.

The soft thump of his heart underneath his skin was a reminder that he was still alive.

He was still fighting.

And so would she.

THE HOURS PASSED BY SLOWLY.

Every now and again, Xul would make a sound but he still had not regained full consciousness.

Athena did the only thing she could think of doing. She held him.

It was the only thing she could do.

She couldn't leave to go search for more flowers till morning and she had no water to clean his wounds.

The night was long and lonely.

Finally, as the twin suns rose slowly in the sky, Athena lifted her pounding head.

The air was cold and she moved the barrier to peek outside.

She could see footprints in the sand of things that had passed by them in the night. The entire time, she had lain with her eyes open, gripping Xul's spear, but none of the animals had tried to enter.

Maybe they thought the zehmip was still alive and they were being digested inside.

Whatever the reason, she was just glad they hadn't been attacked.

As she pushed out her head beyond the barrier, a fat raindrop fell smack into her face. Mildly startled, a slow laugh shook through her frame.

For once, something was going their way.

Pulling the zehmip skin from underneath Xul, she tied the ends together to create a sort of bag.

Taking his spear, she exited the tent and drove it deep into the sand. With the rope, she attached the bag to the spear and tied the other side to the tent.

The raindrops began falling as suddenly as they had begun the first time and Athena ducked back into the tent, leaving the barrier open so she could see what was happening.

Xul groaned again and she ran a hand over his cheek.

"You're going to be okay," she whispered. "I am here with you."

It didn't take long for the makeshift bag to be filled with water and Athena made to exit the tent to gather it.

But, looking down at herself, she decided to strip her clothes off.

It was going to get cold later. She'd need dry clothes.

The cold bit into her skin immediately, and Athena took in a deep breath.

As she pulled the bag inside the tent, she held it in one hand and began washing the sand from his wounds.

It was a slow process but she could already see that it was working.

The only problem was that she was removing the flower sap in the process as well.

One problem at a time, Athena.

You can do this.

His wounds were clean but the rain was still falling hard. With the sand no longer covering him, she realized that he was hurt more than she had first realized.

If she didn't do something soon, he was going to die.

Brushing the thought from her mind, she pulled his head into her lap and cradled it there.

Looking down at him now, she wondered what she'd been afraid of before.

He was just a man. Not some scary alien who was out to get her.

Tracing a finger along his face, she bent her head to rest her forehead against his.

"...thena..."

It was a croak and Athena lifted her head so sharply that it caused pain to shoot down her spine.

"Xul?"

His eyelids were fluttering low as if he was trying to wake up and a rush of joy spread through her.

"Ath..."

He was calling her name.

As tears sprung into her eyes, she held him closer. "Yes, yes, I'm here. Don't talk. I'm here."

The tears were running down her cheeks onto his forehead but she didn't care.

He was trying to raise his hand and she realized the compass-like device was wrapped around it.

"Take..." His green eyes finally opened enough for him to look at her and she could see the life slowly leaving them. They weren't that intense green that she was used to.

"Take...Go...outpost," he said.

The horror of what he was asking her to do hit her like a brick.

"No." Athena swallowed hard and glanced out of the tent. The rain was easing up now. It was her window to go and fetch more flowers. "Don't you dare suggest that."

She wasn't going to do that. She wouldn't leave him.

He was all she had in this godforsaken wilderness but it wasn't even because of that. There was something else that was pushing her to work so hard to keep him alive. Something that was budding within her that she didn't want to analyze.

Resting his head back against the sand, Athena limped out of the tent and grabbed his spear.

Fixing back the barrier in place, she headed down to fetch the flowers.

19

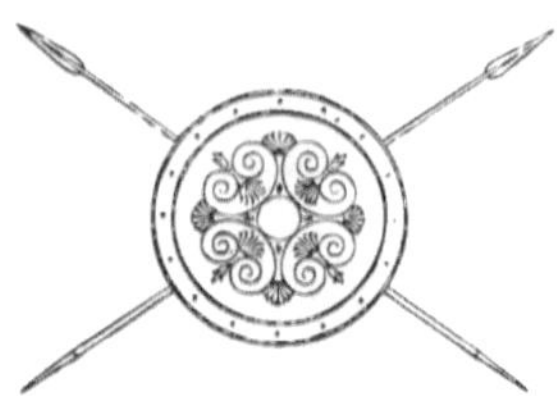

The trek to the flowers seemed twice as long as before but Athena pushed forward, her body protesting with every step.

She was able to gather twice as many flowers as before, though, before heading back to the camp. When she'd reached the cave, she'd expected the gator-guards' bodies to still be lying around but from what it looked like, they'd been torn to pieces by beasts in the night.

The scene made her shiver.

As she pulled herself over the hill and caught sight of the camp where she'd left Xul, her blood ran cold.

Close by were two of those invisible snake-dragon things, only their dark scales were showing now so she could see them. They weren't attacking, though, but because of their huge size, she could see them clearly from so far away.

What were they doing so close?

Gripping the spear, she crept forward slowly and something else caught her attention.

There were little beings, maybe six or so of them, all circling the tent.

They were dressed in little robes that were the color of the sand and they had little round bald heads.

They were brown too, almost the color of the sand but of various degrees of brown.

As she approached, one of them saw her and began muttering wildly to the others in its language.

Spear poised, she approached warily and all the little men whipped out what looked like little spears of their own.

Great.

One of them said something to her and Athena frowned.

Tapping her ears, she said, "I cannot understand you."

Maybe the damn translator thing wasn't working.

The little alien repeated whatever it had said and pointed at the spear in her hand.

Oh, it wanted her to surrender while they had their spears pointed at her?

Hell. No.

From the way they looked, she assumed they were the residents of Muk. And, apparently, they didn't take kindly to strangers around these parts.

One of them poked the side of Invisible Dragon Numero Uno and the thing roared down at her.

Ok then.

Message received.

As she let the spear fall from her hand slowly, she realized she hadn't noticed the small seats that dotted the dragon beast.

They rode that thing?

Second message received.

Don't mess with bitches who could tame bitches who'd almost fucked you up.

As the spear fell, the little aliens seemed satisfied and the one who'd poked the dragon beast patted the animal, which promptly settled its head in the sand.

They were speaking to her again, their spears now lowered, and were pointing to her bloodied clothes.

One of them pulled open the barrier way too easily and stepped inside.

"No!" Athena moved after the thing but the others raised their spears at her again.

Glancing at the dragon beast, she swallowed hard.

This was not good. This was not good at all.

More mumbling ensued.

Their language sounded like a series of clicks and whistles and the one inside must be telling them about Xul because, for a second, they all ran to the entrance and forgot all about her.

Glancing back at the spear, she wondered if she should grab it but the dragon thing had its eyes on her. She wasn't sure if it would act on its own accord but she wasn't sure it was worth it to take the chance either.

One of the little men approached her, reaching only to her knee, and poked her with the butt of its spear.

Athena winced.

It had chosen to poke exactly where the wound was on her leg.

The thing's little beady eyes widened slightly and the innocent response made her wonder if it was a child.

Its size certainly suggested it was.

It grabbed her hand and spotted the flowers then it started speaking to the others again.

From inside the tent, she heard the others reply to it.

Then the thing tried to pull the flowers from her hand, but she held on to them.

It was the only thing she knew would help Xul. She wasn't about to just give it up. But the little beady eyes focused on hers and the little alien pressed the sharp part of its spear against her chest.

"Fine," Athena said through gritted teeth.

God-fucking-damn this planet.

The little alien grabbed the flowers, threw them in its mouth, and began chewing.

"I need those!" Athena screamed at it, her hands balled into fists.

Glancing back at the spear, she wondered if she could take them.

Probably she could but not with two dragon beasts close by.

As the thing chewed, it rushed toward the tent and Athena followed behind.

When she entered, her eyes widened at the sight that greeted her.

They were all spitting saliva in their little hands and rubbing it into Xul's wounds.

"No!" Athena screamed but one of them raised its spear toward her.

Ignoring it, she stepped forward, ready to pull them one after the other off of his body when another raised its spear at her.

In a split second, the little alien vaulted itself on her body and held the spear at her throat.

Fuck.

Fuck, fuck, fuck.

She wasn't about to let them just prep him for their meal.

What the hell was wrong with this planet?

But as the anger boiled in her veins, she noticed the one who had taken the flowers from her was now spitting the chewed up flowers into its hand and massaging the soft mixture into Xul's wounds.

Wait...they weren't trying to hurt him. They were trying to help him.

The little alien looked up at her when it was done and said something to her.

"I can't understand you...do you want more?" She looked around at them, her gaze bouncing off each of their faces.

They all looked alike. It was strange as hell. The only thing that made them look slightly different was the fact that they were different shades of brown.

Raising her hands in the air, her gaze locked with the one that had jumped on her chest. Dark beady eyes blinked at her but it seemed as if it understood that she was saying she wouldn't resist for it hopped back to the floor.

Reaching into her bosom, Athena pulled out a large wad of flowers. She didn't have pockets and it had been the best way to carry as much as she could.

What sounded like a murmur of approval echoed through the

group and they all took some and began chewing on the petals. Soon, they were daubing the mixture of their saliva and the fluid from the petals into Xul's wounds.

Turning him on his back, they did the same thing to the wounds there.

Athena swallowed hard as she saw the deep gashes across his back. Even his light-brown hair was dyed a deep red by his own blood.

When the little men finished, one of them said something to her and Athena shook her head. She couldn't understand a word they were saying and she assumed they couldn't understand her either.

It turned to mumble something to its friends and the others seemed to nod in agreement.

"Ok, you just agreed on something. What did you agree on?"

The little beings ignored her as they stood around Xul's body, three on each side.

Before she could protest, the beings heaved and lifted him above their heads.

"Wait, no!" Athena was brushed out of the way. "Where are you taking him?"

As the dragon beast saw them approach, it flattened itself on the sand as they climbed on top of it, still carrying Xul above their heads.

Dashing over to Xul's spear, Athena grabbed it and turned on them but the dragon beast roared at her, causing her to jump back.

Shit.

This couldn't be happening.

Where were they taking him?

They put him to recline on of the seats and looked at her, as if expecting her to do something.

"What do you want? Where are you taking him?"

One of the little aliens patted the seat beside Xul and pointed to her.

"Ok, you want me to get on?"

Muttering some more, the little alien pointed behind her.

Turning, to look in the distance, Athena's eyes widened slightly.

This planet...

It was like a brown wall was some way off. That only meant one thing.

Sandstorm.

The little alien patted the seat again, this time not as softly as before.

As if she had a choice.

They had Xul, and a sandstorm was heading their way.

Climbing up on to the dragon beast was not easy, she kept slipping and one of the little men had to pull her up.

As it held on to her hand, though, she realized its skin had a sort of suction.

"Unfair advantage," she muttered and she settled beside Xul.

He still looked unresponsive and she hoped the medicine was working.

She more than hoped.

She prayed.

As the little aliens settled on the dragon beasts, the creatures lifted their bodies and started gliding over the sand.

It wasn't long before she realized they were heading down towards the wreckage of the Isclit ship.

As they reached the carnage, the little men began murmuring excitedly.

Athena glanced around, trying to ignore the pain in her head.

Either they liked the carnage or something else excited them.

They came to stop at what remained of the ship and their excited murmurs grew.

As they hopped off and began circling the wreckage, Athena turned her eyes on Xul.

The flower concoction was dissolving into his wounds and she assumed that was a good thing.

With one of her hands, she smoothed the hair off his brow.

He was going to be okay.

She was sure of it.

A loud sound caught her attention and she realized the six little men were lifting the entire ship, hoisting it high above their shoulders and bringing it over to the other dragon beast.

With a series of mumbling, they secured the ship onto the beast with rope before mounting the beast again.

Soon, they were moving.

Glancing behind them, Athena could see the sandstorm moving closer.

At least they weren't heading in that direction.

20

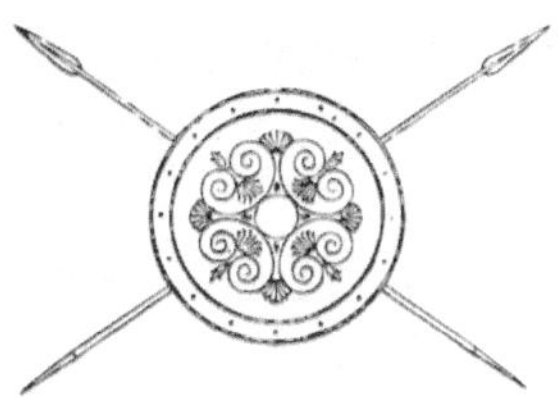

It was almost dark when they stopped in front of tall walls that looked like they were made of...glass?

A little alien standing on what looked like a tower shouted something to the group and one of them replied, waving its arms about to some other alien she could not see.

Soon, the gates were opened and their little party entered.

There were little men everywhere. All dressed the same. All looking alike.

As soon as the dragon beasts stopped, they were surrounded and excited mumbling ensued.

It was evident the little men she'd traveled with were telling the others what had happened and though some of them were looking at her they all seemed more interested in Xul and the spaceship wreckage.

A feeling of possessiveness hit her out of nowhere, and she held him to her closely.

One of them was looking at the spear as well but at least they weren't all pulling out their weapons to point at her.

They were mumbling things she could not understand when one of them turned to her and said something.

Athena shook her head. "I can't understand you."

The little alien kept mumbling anyway and pointed to Xul then further into the camp.

As she looked where the little arm pointed to, she realized there was a network of small holes all around the camp.

The one that had been talking to her said something to the others and suddenly there was a flurry around them.

Some were unloading the wrecked spaceship and others were busy lifting Xul off the seat. Grabbing his spear, Athena lowered herself and tried to ignore the pain shooting through her body.

It wasn't time to collapse now.

The little aliens seemed good enough but you never knew with these guys. They were inhabitants on a planet that couldn't be trusted. Maybe they were the same.

She followed behind them, feeling like a giant, and they approached one of the little holes networked into the camp. Stooping as she entered, she was glad she wasn't claustrophobic but the cave opened up into a large room and she was able to stand upright without bumping her head.

Around them, zehmip skins lined one section, which she assumed was the bed because that was where they took Xul.

Simple furnishings made of glass dotted the little room and above them, what looked like little glowing worms were wriggling in a glass orb, shedding light in the room.

The little men rested Xul and hustled out of the room.

Athena glanced around and went to lie by him.

His eyes were still closed but the petals had all dissolved into his wounds and they looked considerably less angry.

Athena's shoulders shook as she released a sigh and rested her head against his chest, taking comfort in the slow rise and fall as he breathed.

She felt drained, as if she wouldn't be able to move even in she tried and, as if her body took note of the fact that she wasn't fighting for life at the moment, her consciousness waned.

She was out of energy.

If she could just close her eyes.

Just for a little. She wouldn't sleep. She'd just rest them.

Just for a little.

SOMETHING SOFT WAS NESTLED against him, their little arm draped across his chest and their bare cheek against his skin.

Xul's eyes fluttered open and he glanced around the room.

Was he dreaming?

He knew these walls well. Only one place in the galaxy looked like this.

He was at the outpost. How did he get to the outpost?

Lifting his head proved painful but he did it anyway. She was nestled against him, still caked in sand, dirt, and blood.

Glancing down at himself, he noticed his wounds had been tended to, the sand removed, and healing petals crushed and placed into every gash.

Brushing a bit of her hair off her face, he gazed down into her face.

He had bits and pieces of memory of her pulling him from where he'd fallen, crawling on her hands and knees as she struggled to get them both to safety.

Anyone else would have just left him there for dead. But not this human. She'd fought to pull him out of danger even though doing so had risked her own life.

The only other people he had in the universe who would do such a thing for him were his brothers in the Restitution—the men he fought with; the same men who were stuck on an Isclit ship going through hell to see this mission through.

He only had them.

And now he had her.

She was smart and strong. Stronger than he could have ever imagined and now he wished he could take back all the times he'd teased her about being weak.

It took great strength to do what she did.

As his eyes roved over her, he felt a pain in his chest.

She hadn't even tended to herself. He could see that her wounds were still open, some still bleeding.

Glancing toward the exit, he let out a soft whistle and rested his head back down.

Qrak.

The little exertion of just raising himself had made him woozy.

It only took a few seconds for one of the Mukkians to walk into the room. Its little beady eyes blinked at Xul and when it realized he was awake, it rushed out of the room.

A few more seconds later, it returned with a friend and skins with water and food.

"Xul," one said. "It has been many suns since we last saw you. We have been awaiting your return."

He knew they were referring to him sending word from the outpost but that would have to wait.

"You must heal her."

They blinked at him, then looked at Athena.

"Heal her?" One blinked at the other. "Your captor?"

Xul frowned, then a low rumble began in his chest.

It hurt to laugh but he couldn't help but chuckle.

"She is not my captor. She is my..."

What was she? His friend? The woman who'd appeared in his life and began awakening something in him that he never knew was there?

The Mukkians blinked.

"She is under my care. Heal her," he said.

The Mukkians nodded and disappeared from the cave.

Brushing her hair back, Xul whispered her name, "Athena?"

She didn't respond and he didn't expect her to.

Her body had gone past its limit.

What she needed now was rest.

The Mukkians reentered with bowls filled with freshly ground healing flowers and warm water.

He watched as they lifted her off him and he immediately missed the feel of her body on his.

They lay her beside him and proceeded to clean her wounds and apply the healing salve.

"There are wounds all over No Horn's body. Shall we strip her to heal them?" One Mukkian tilted its head toward Xul, waiting for an answer.

A soft smile smoothed his lips. He didn't think she was going to like that name.

"Do what you must. My only concern is that she lives."

The Mukkians went back to work, stripping Athena of her clothes and cleaning the rest of her body as they applied the salve to her wounds.

If it was any other species, he'd have been wary of them having their hands roving over her naked body, but the Mukkians were so sexless, he never thought of them as ever harboring hedonistic thoughts. When they finished and left the room, Xul turned his head so he could look at her.

Before, he'd forced himself not to, but now...

This little female had pulled him. She'd fought beside him. She'd saved his life.

Something felt strange inside his chest and he realized it was his heart.

His heart was yearning.

Taking a breath that made his body shudder, he stretched his hand and took her small one into his.

He was feeling things.

Things he didn't know he would ever be able to feel.

Athena.

Athena from Earth.

What had she done?

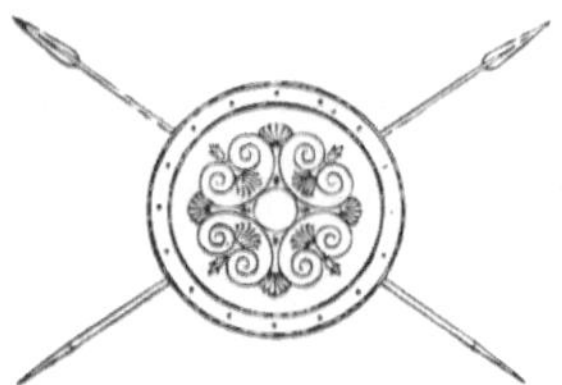

Athena's eyes fluttered open.

Something was different.

Her entire body didn't ache anymore and, from the cool breeze that was tickling her skin, she knew she was naked.

Again.

As she tried to lift her head to look around, a headache that felt like a migraine crashed into her skull.

Ok, so maybe no head movements.

"You should rest." The deep voice that floated so close to her ears made something jump with happiness inside her.

Turning her head to the side, she couldn't help but smile at him.

"You're awake."

"I am."

Something clouded her vision and she realized it was her own tears. It was immediate, as if she'd been bottling the emotion so much that the mere realization that he was going to be ok let the floodgates burst.

As the first teardrop fell, the rest followed in quick succession and she couldn't stop them.

He was alive.

He'd made it.

"You are not happy that I am?" He used a finger to wipe away her tears and she grabbed onto his hand and held on to it, nodding as she did.

"I am. I'm just..." Athena gulped. "I'm relieved." Wiping her tears, she cursed at herself.

"I am here because of you," Xul said, frowning as more tears came from her eyes.

"Oh, Xul," she mumbled beneath the tears. "You have no idea..."

Oh, but he did.

Xul watched her, bewildered, unsure of what to do. Then he did the one thing that he thought would help.

Tilting her chin up, he touched his lips against hers and for that moment, as their lips touched, time stood still.

It was just she and him alone in the universe.

Something strong resonated within her and she wondered if he felt it too.

Xul's warm breath brushed over her face as their eyes met, neither of them moving. His intense green was against her blue, and what she saw in his eyes was something she couldn't quite comprehend.

A sound like a low growl vibrated in his chest as he ran his tongue over her bottom lip and Athena closed her eyes.

"So sweet," he murmured. "Like the nectar from the sweetest *kioju* tree."

She didn't know what that meant but she knew exactly how he felt. He tasted intoxicating, like she wouldn't be able to get enough—ever—and this was with just a brush of his lips.

She felt a moan shudder through his frame as she opened herself to him.

Pulling her into his arms, Xul tried to hold her lightly, not wanting to upset her wounds. But she was kissing him back as if she didn't want him to let go and her eagerness only lit a fire within him that he wasn't sure he wanted to put out.

Flipping her on her back, he braced himself over her as his tongue played with hers, loving the feel of its soft smoothness against his.

She wrapped her arms around his neck and pulled him closer, moaning into his mouth as she pulled him toward her.

Qrak.

If she kept doing that he was going to have to take her...and he wasn't sure if she wanted that or was even ready for it.

Was he ready for it?

Running his fingers down the side of her smooth body, he circled one of her breasts and then held one in his palm as he kneaded it underneath his fingers.

Athena moaned again and nipped at his upper lip, causing him to press her deeper into the zehmip skins as he ravished her mouth.

As he broke the kiss and ran his mouth down her slender neck, a burning need seemed to engulf him.

He needed her. Needed to feel her.

As his tongue flicked over her nipple, Athena arched her back and gasped, causing another one of those growls to rumble in his chest.

She was responsive and he liked that but it was only making him want her more and he wasn't sure he was going to be able to stop if they kept going on.

As he took her nipple into his mouth and played with the little bud between his lips, her soft little cries made him groan again.

"Athena," he growled.

"Xul," she said, her eyes fluttering open and he raised his head.

As their eyes met, Athena exhaled a ragged breath.

She knew what that look in his eyes was now.

It was need. Pure, unbridled need.

He was running his eyes down her body now, slowly, taking in every inch of her as if he had never seen her naked before, and Athena squirmed underneath his gaze.

She'd never had a man look at her quite like that before. It was a wild, primitive, possessive sort of look that made something within her respond.

"Athena," Xul growled again, as his gaze stopped at her center. She saw him gulp before looking back at her in the eyes.

"My body is telling me to do things..." His voice was coarse and it was as if he was fighting some sort of internal battle.

"Then do it..." Athena breathed.

His eyes fell back to her folds again as he leaned in close, burying his face in the softness of her inner thigh.

Athena closed her eyes and dipped her head back and Xul raised himself above her again.

As his fingers parted her folds, she felt him pause and she opened her eyes.

He was looking at her strangely and she felt the urge to slam her legs shut.

"What's this?" he murmured.

"It's my—" Athena gasped as he ran a finger over her clit and Xul raised an eyebrow. Brushing his finger over her clit again caused the same response and a twinkle lit up his eyes.

"It is the center of your pleasure," he murmured, dipping his head to run his tongue over her throbbing bud.

Athena gripped the zehmip coat beneath them and inhaled deeply.

As he ran his tongue over her one more time, Xul murmured, "The women of my people do not have such a pleasure spot."

Athena opened her mouth to answer but all that came out was a low moan as she felt Xul cup her fully, covering her folds with his mouth.

His tongue was heavy and slick and as he licked her, he ran the underside of it over her clit. There were ridges under there that made her eyes flutter back in her head.

"Oh God," she breathed, reaching down to hold on to his horns.

Xul glanced up at her with a satisfied gleam in his eyes as he lapped at her juices.

She was moaning and writhing against his tongue now and it

only made him hunger for her more. Her arousal was intoxicating, pulling him in. He felt consumed by her need and it was feeding his own fire within.

"Oh fuck." Athena's back arched high as she felt his thick, slick tongue slip between her lips and deep inside her. She could feel her breathing accelerating as if she was running on a track and that was just because of his tongue.

Maybe it was because she hadn't had sex in a while but his tongue felt glorious.

As he began to pump it deep within her, Xul raised his hands to cup her breasts, kneading the nipples between his fingers.

Her orgasm crashed into her suddenly and hard, her body trembling as she held on to his horns to steady herself. And, as her breathing slowed, Athena opened her eyes to look down.

Xul was lifting his head now, his mouth glistening with her juices and his eyes alight with need.

She could see something bounce beneath his loincloth and her gaze fell to the spot.

Xul followed where she was looking and a slow frown suddenly creased his forehead.

"What is it?" Athena whispered.

Xul took a while to answer as he watched her warily. "I have just realized I may be different from your human lovers..." He trailed off, easing back on his haunches.

Athena raised herself into a sitting position, as her gaze raked over him. The wounds on his body were still pink but apart from that he looked perfect.

Big, wild, and perfect.

As she ran her tongue over her bottom lip, she saw Xul swallow hard and his package twitched again underneath his loincloth.

"Let me see," Athena whispered.

Xul's eyes widened slightly, watching her as she crawled forward. But he didn't stop her when she grasped the loincloth and pulled it away.

When she gasped and looked up at him, concern was in his eyes as he searched her face.

Athena took him into her hands, her mouth falling open slightly.

"Good God," she breathed.

Nestled between his thick leg muscles, was the biggest, thickest cock she had ever seen in her life.

He was massive. She reckoned he was no less than eleven inches with impressive girth to go along with it.

Xul was still watching her strangely as she ran her hand along the length of him.

"Wow," she breathed.

There was no way he was going to fit inside her but to say she wasn't attracted to what she was seeing like a magnet, she'd be lying to herself.

There was a network of veins along his cock, forming deep ridges that made her pussy twitch just looking at them. She could just imagine how good they felt.

His mushroom tip was wider than any she'd ever seen, the skin on it soft and thick.

It called to her and Athena leaned forward tentatively to run her tongue over it.

She heard Xul's breath catch in his throat but he didn't stop her. As she covered the tip with her mouth, it pushed past her lips and she ran her tongue around it.

Moisture from his tip fell on her tongue as she sucked on him and Athena moaned as the taste filled her mouth.

It was not like any precum she'd ever tasted before.

It wasn't salty.

Instead, it tasted like citrus.

It only made her suck on him harder and she felt his body tense as a low moan rumbled through him.

Pushing him as far as she could down her throat, she stopped just before gagging, her eyes widening when she realized how much of him was still in her hands.

As she pumped the length of him, Xul clasped her head between his hands, his eyes burning green as he watched her mouth move over him.

"Damn," Athena breathed as she slid him out of her mouth. He jerked in her hand as she stared at him, enthralled by the sheer size of it.

"Just how..." she breathed.

"Just how what?" Xul's voice was hoarse and he inhaled sharply as she ran a finger from his tip right down his shaft.

"How does this fit into the women of your kind?"

Xul paused, his expression changing to slight amusement.

"I'll show you," he growled as he pushed her back against the zehmip coat.

Their eyes locked as he climbed over her, his gaze never leaving hers as he settled between her legs.

Bending his head, Xul nuzzled his face into her neck and his hands went down beneath her and settled underneath her hips.

As he grasped her ass in his palms, he bit her neck lightly.

"Relax for me," he whispered, and Athena nodded. But her heart was hammering in her chest almost to the beat of the pulsing going on between her legs.

She wasn't tense because this was something she was unsure of. She was tense because she wanted it so bad.

God, she wanted to feel him.

She wanted to feel him now.

When his mushroom tip hit her entrance, Athena bit her bottom lip and swallowed hard.

"So small," Xul whispered, as he pushed against her entrance. As his mushroom popped in, his low growl vibrated against her.

"So tight."

Athena gripped his shoulders, as she swiveled her hips slightly, allowing herself to get accustomed to his width.

"Fuck," she whispered. Her pussy was throbbing with pleasure and this wasn't even the length of him. "Fuck," she breathed again.

Xul lifted his head slightly over hers, staring deeply into her eyes as he pulled her hips toward him, sliding deeper into her folds.

"Xul," Athena breathed, her arms wrapping around his neck.

As he began to pump slowly, his intense gaze was on her, watching her every movement, her every reaction, and Athena opened to him, letting him take her.

It felt like he was splitting her in two. It was a feeling like none ever before—that undeniable feeling of being completely and utterly filled. She was stretched to the limit and she clenched around him, hanging on to him and he slid into her warm wetness.

The feeling was building within her slowly and again she felt as if it was only him and her in the entire universe.

This wasn't just fucking.

It wasn't mindless sex.

There was more to this.

Much more.

As Xul's lips crashed into hers, another orgasm rocked through her, making her tremble against him, her body shaking uncontrollably as he held her close.

He quickened his thrusts then, her orgasm making her even wetter, and soon he was groaning against her mouth.

"Xul," she murmured and, with a growl, he stiffened, biting down softly on her bottom lip and his cock jerked within her.

She could feel the thick streams of his release shooting deep within her, making her tingle with delight.

When the pulses finally left his body, Xul eased up over her, his gaze searching her face.

"Did I hurt you?"

Athena chuckled, dropping her head back against the zehmip skins.

"No. The opposite."

He seemed to like that answer as he rolled to the side, pulling her along with him.

She was very aware that he was still buried deep within her but it only made everything more intimate.

As he settled her against him, Xul snuggled his face in her hair.

"You smell nice," he murmured.

Athena smiled.

There was a new feeling fluttering in her chest and she wasn't quite sure what it was.

All she knew was that it felt good.

And she wanted to feel it again and again and again.

22

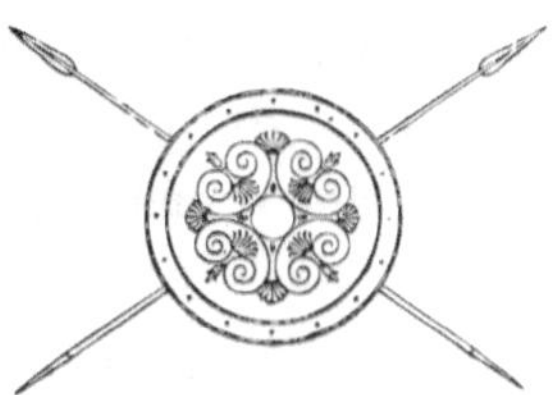

When she woke, she was still nestled against Xul.

Something smelling like food wafted into her nostrils and she turned slightly, her eyes adjusting to the dim light.

All around them were little alien men standing with what looked like trays upon trays of food.

Their little beady eyes were focused on either her or Xul, she wasn't quite sure. They had no irises, it seemed. It was difficult to tell where they were looking when they weren't turning their heads.

"Um, Xul." She nudged the body of the hulk beside her but soon realized he was already awake.

He said something to them in their language and soon the little men were placing the trays down before shuffling out of the room.

"You can understand them?"

Xul seemed to smile. He still had his hand draped around her and her cheeks grew warm when she felt his meat resting against her leg.

"Yes, I speak Mukkish," he said.

"My translator thing doesn't pick up anything they say." Athena touched behind her ear where the Isclit had administered the shot.

Closing her eyes, she took a few breaths. It was hard to concentrate when she could feel the weight of his dick against her leg.

Just hours before, that weight had been pumping deep inside her.

"No. The Isclit translator wouldn't have most of the lesser-known tongues in its database. Muk is a planet that is considered...futile." His eyes were moving slowly over her face as he studied her and Athena felt herself blushing again as his cock jerked against her leg.

Clearing her throat, she gestured to the surrounding trays.

"What's this?"

"Supper. You must eat." He released her somewhat reluctantly and stretched for one of the trays, setting it down in front of her.

It looked like roasted chicken dipped in deep gravy but she was sure it was anything but that. Her stomach growled in protest as if it didn't care.

Glancing at her naked belly, Xul frowned.

"Have that by yourself," he said, his gaze rising to fall on her nipples.

Athena flushed again.

Goddammit. She wasn't going to survive much longer blushing like some kind of schoolgirl.

Grabbing one of the zehmip skins, she wrapped the coat around herself, noting Xul's amused expression.

"Why do you cover? I have been to your most secret place."

Athena gave him a look but she couldn't stop the smile that spread across her lips.

For the first time since this whole ordeal began, she felt...good.

Breaking a piece of the meat off the tray, she popped it into her mouth and chewed.

A burst of flavor spread over her tongue.

"Mmm. What is this?" She tore off another piece and popped it into her mouth.

Xul frowned as he looked at the tray. "Sand frog, I assume."

Athena spat the thing out so quickly, it shot across the room, to Xul's surprise.

Wiping her mouth, she eyed the tray and pushed it away.

"What's that one?" She pointed at another tray with meat on it.

"Arbiran lizard," Xul said, watching her, amused.

Athena frowned. "And that one?" She pointed at another.

"Sand-cat," Xul said.

"I'll have that one then," Athena said, stretching for the tray. Maybe it was because she was starving but the meat tasted damn good. It beat eating zehmip flesh any day.

"You do not eat frogs on your planet?" Xul asked as he bit into whatever was on his tray. She dared not ask what it was.

"Some people do," Athena answered.

"Tell me about your planet."

Their gazes locked and Athena frowned.

"What do you want to know? You didn't seem so interested in me before."

There was a pause, then he finally said. "I'm curious...about you."

There seemed to be more behind what he said but Athena decided not to ask. Whatever he was feeling was probably mutual.

"My planet is filled with beautiful, vast oceans, filled with a whole set of different species and biomes. On land, we have massive forests, lakes, rivers, animals, and people, lots of people. We have skyscrapers, and cars, and," she looked down at herself, "malls to buy clothes and shoes..."

Talking about Earth made it seem far, far away, as if she was never going to see it again.

"When will we continue on to the outpost?" She raised her eyes to his and found that he'd stopped eating and was watching her intently.

"We are at the outpost."

The piece of meat she'd been eating fell from her fingers.

"We are?" She glanced around the room. "So what now?"

"I have already sent the message to command."

"When did you do that?"

"While you were sleeping," he said.

"Oh."

So that meant things were already in motion.

"So what now? How do we get back on the ship and what happens when we get there?"

Xul's face hardened. "We will set the bombs to blow up the ship."

"Then?"

"Then we will escape to the Elysium."

"Elysium. What's that?"

"That's the name of our base."

A sliver of excitement ran through her. "And that's where we'll be able to send a message to Earth?"

Something crossed behind his eyes and he took a few seconds to answer.

"Yes."

"I sense there's something you're not telling me."

Xul raised an eyebrow slightly then bit into the meat in his hand.

"We are millions of light years away from your planet. The Isclit ship took a wormhole shortly after abducting your people. We are on the other side of the galaxy."

Something inside of her fell but she wasn't going to give up hope.

"So, you're saying our message might never reach Earth."

"No, your message will reach." Xul blinked.

It took a few seconds for what he was trying to say to dawn on her.

"But we are so far away they might not be able to help us..." She trailed off, feeling a part of her die inside.

"I doubt it," he answered.

"What about borrowing a ship and going through the wormhole?" Hope flared in her eyes.

Xul's gaze sank. "The wormhole closed shortly after we came through it. According to the ship's log, it only opens once in every twenty million of your Earth years."

Well, that explained the saber-toothed tiger and the T-Rex that had been on board.

They visited Earth every now and again and stored whatever species they could find.

Suddenly, red hot anger coursed through her veins as tears stung at her eyes.

"You're telling me I'm stranded here! Why did you tell me that I could send a message if you knew there was no chance of ever returning to Earth! Why did you give me hope?!"

He didn't answer her for what felt like ages and she watched him fight with his emotions behind his eyes.

"Because, Athena," he finally said. "You had nothing. Hope was all you had left."

Her anger flared as she slid off the zehmip skins and glared at him.

"Then why tell me now! What do I have now?!"

Xul's gaze settled on hers with clarity.

"Now," he said, "you have me."

SHE WAS STANDING on top of the perimeter wall at one of the lookout spots, staring out into the desert. Her arms were folded across her chest, holding tight the zehmip coat that she'd draped around her soft body to hide herself.

Seeing her standing there now, defiance radiating through her bones, he felt a sense of pride he was sure was misplaced.

But it was there nonetheless, feeding something within him that made him damn well impressed with the little alien who'd crashed in his life so suddenly.

And he hadn't been joking when he'd told her that she had him.

He felt a sense of...possessiveness for her that he didn't know had been growing.

Below her, she paid no attention to the Mukkians who were chattering wildly and pointing up at her.

As he walked toward her, his muscles ached underneath his skin but the discomfort would ease long before the vessel arrived for them to head back to the Isclit's ship.

Brushing past the Mukkians, he climbed the ladder up the wall.

From what he could hear, the little aliens were debating if they should climb the wall and get her to come down by force.

As he came to stand beside her, she didn't acknowledge his presence.

Instead, she kept staring out into the desert.

On her face, dried tears decorated her cheeks, etched on her skin by the dry sand that was blowing in the air.

"This must be...hard for you," he finally said.

Athena didn't answer.

"Do you have...a loved one, on Earth?"

Athena swallowed a sad chuckle.

"If you're asking me if I have a boyfriend waiting for me at home, then no." She glared at him. "That is not why I want to go back so badly." She turned to look back out into the desert.

"Then why?"

Athena gulped, remaining silent for a few seconds. "Because I am alone." She drew in a ragged breath. "You have no idea how that feels."

Xul turned to stare out into the desert as well, before replying, "I know exactly how it feels."

Athena glanced at him, a slight frown on her forehead, as she waited for him to continue.

"I am alone too."

"Your planet is far away?"

"Yes."

"Can you reach it?"

"Yes."

Athena's frown deepened so much she could feel it hurting her head. "Then that's not exactly the same thing, then, is it?"

Her mouth setting into a hard line, she made to turn back to stare into the distance when she felt herself being pulled towards him.

Xul had his arms around her, as he turned her to face him.

"I have a planet. But I have no home. I lost everything. Everything I cared about when the Isclit's ravaged my planet for the High Tasqals. I have nothing there."

The pain flooding his eyes made her swallow hard.

"I'm sorry," Athena whispered, suddenly feeling selfish.

Everybody had demons following them...only hers was standing right next to her and she was attracted to him.

"Come with me," Xul said, his eyes searching hers.

"Come with you?" Athena repeated.

"Come with me after the mission. We don't have to be alone."

Athena blinked, digesting his words as they repeated in her head.

The murmuring of the Mukkians grew louder and Xul looked down at them.

"They are telling me to take you off the wall by force," he said. "You are too tall to be standing up here. You stand out."

Athena rolled her eyes and looked down at the little aliens. Sure enough, they were all chattering and looking at her.

"So they aren't concerned about you? You're almost twice my size."

Xul smiled a little. "They think I'm here to take you down," he said, then added, "By force."

"Oh really. And are you?"

Xul shrugged. "Not if you comply."

"I'd like to see you try." As soon as she said it, she wished she hadn't, as that same amused expression spread over his features.

In one smooth movement, he swept her off her feet and threw her over his shoulders.

"I can walk, you know!"

"I know. But this gives me a much nicer view."

Athena flushed, very aware that her rump was nestled by his head.

As he took her down the ladder, the Mukkians stopped murmuring and walked away. He was carrying her back to the cave when he stopped slowly and placed his hand over his ears, his face contorting as he set her down.

"What is it?" Athena searched his face for clues, watching in horror as he sank to his knees, both of his hands covering his ears.

"Xul! What's happening?!" She clutched him, her gaze darting around the enclosure but none of the little men were to be seen anywhere.

"It's Yce," he said.

"Yce?"

"Something is wrong," he said through gritted teeth. "Something is wrong on the Isclit ship."

23

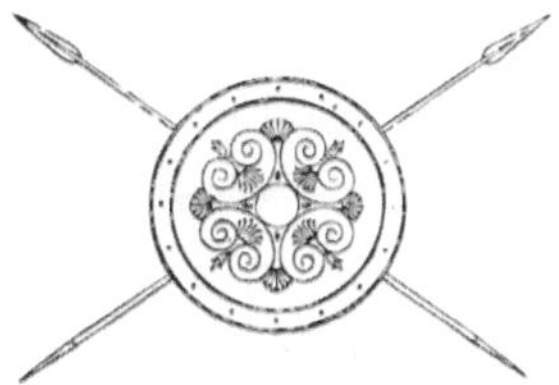

Xul was crumpled on his knees and was rambling.

Well, she assumed he was rambling because nothing he said made sense.

"Stop him..." he groaned out.

He seemed to be talking to himself, having some sort of conversation, and she couldn't quite figure out what he meant by any of it.

"You have to calm him down."

"Calm who down?" For a minute, she wondered if he was referring to himself in the third person, and if so, that didn't creep her out one bit. No, not at all.

"The mission depends on it," he groaned out again, gritting his teeth, veins popping up on his forehead.

Athena's eyes widened as she looked at him, unsure of what to do.

What did you do when your demon appeared to be demon-possessed?

Her demon?

He wasn't her anything. At least...not yet. Was he?

And just as suddenly as it had started, Xul removed his hand from his head and leaned his head back, shaking his head from side to side.

"What the hell was that about?"

Xul's eyes locked with hers.

"I just interfaced with Yce. He's on the Isclit ship."

"Wait, what? You just spoke to someone in space? How?"

"Yce is telepathic. He can connect with almost any being in the universe. However, distance is sometimes a factor."

Athena took a moment to digest that information.

"Did he say anything about the other humans on board? Are they alright?"

Xul nodded. "All humans are...alive."

That didn't sound too positive but she'd take it. "Alive" was better than the other option: dead.

"So who were you telling to calm down?"

Xul's expression became thoughtful. "Crex."

"And who is that? Another of your men?"

"He is a Ceqtaq. Stubborn. Hard to deal with. The most wayward of my men but one of the best fighters," Xul said.

Ceqtaq.

She'd heard that word somewhere before.

Then it came to her.

The High Tasqals that day when she was being auctioned.

They'd mentioned buying Piper to put with a Ceqtaq.

"He's bonded," Xul murmured, still in his thoughts.

"What now?"

"He's bonded. Crex has bonded."

"What do you mean?"

Xul's eyes met hers. "He has bonded with one of your kind and he is about to blow the mission to protect her."

***

XUL WAS PACING in what had been a large enough cave when she'd first seen it. Now, it seemed small with him looming in it.

He'd been frowning since he dropped the bomb about one of his men bonding with one of the female humans and, since then, he'd been pacing and shooting glances her away every now and again.

Athena settled back against the zehmip skins and watched him move.

What the Mukkians had done had been nothing short of a miracle.

His wounds seemed to be healing in front of her very eyes.

She assumed their saliva had some sort of healing properties and regardless of how gross that was, she was thankful for it.

She'd managed to tie the zehmip coat around her in a sort of bandeau dress and as she cut another strip of cloth from the coat to tie her hair back, she stopped as she noticed Xul watching her intently.

"What is it?" she whispered.

Xul stalked over to her and took her chin in his hand, tilting her face up toward his.

"What is it with your kind?" he asked.

"What do you mean?" Athena breathed, his sudden closeness doing things to her insides that she could not comprehend.

"You disarm us. Make us feel things that we have trained ourselves not to feel."

Somehow, it felt as if he was talking about himself, and Athena's gaze fell to his lips.

"Crex has bonded. That is unheard of. And yet, I find myself..." His words trailed off as he looked deep into her eyes. "Your species has the power to bewitch."

The chuckle that bubbled within her seemed to catch him off guard.

"You think I'm bewitching you?" Athena chuckled softly.

"From the very first moment I saw you, my body responded in a way it has never done before," he murmured. Athena's eyebrows rose. This was news to her. "It wasn't just your naked body. It was something else."

Athena slapped his hand from her chin and rolled away from

him. But the thought that he had been attracted to her from even then somehow made her tingle inside.

Xul ignored her efforts to get away and climbed on the skins over to her, grasping her hands as he pinned her down, frowning at her.

"What is it about you?" He studied her face.

Athena mimicked his frown. "I can assure you, I am not putting some spell on you."

"Oh, but you are…" Xul's gaze dropped to her breasts, which were now pushing up over the tight bandeau.

Xul let go of her hands as he dipped his head to her neck, nipping her skin lightly.

A soft moan escaped her lips, matched by a low one of his own.

"I want you," he growled. "Now."

He was just about to rip the dress away from her bosom when three little Mukkians rushed into the room, babbling incoherently.

Xul froze, his face hardening immediately.

"It is here," he said.

"What is?" Athena breathed, trying to still the fire that had begun to burn within her.

"The Elysium."

WHEN THEY EXITED THE CAVE, the little men were bustling about excitedly.

Air was swirling around within the camp, similar to how air moved in the direct vicinity of a helicopter. But Athena could see no such craft or vessel.

All the little Mukkians were looking up into the sky at something apparently she alone could not see.

Frowning, Athena looked around her.

Xul stepped in front of her and looked up. In the next few seconds, a large starship appeared out of nowhere.

It was a sleek white that reflected the light of the twin suns.

It was huge, almost covering the entire camp and as it hovered above them, Xul reached back and held her hand in his, glancing back at her as he did so.

"Is this your ship?" she said over the wind.

Xul nodded as a staircase materialized in front of them.

He said something to the Mukkians in their tongue then led her aboard the ship.

The stairs seemed to hover in midair, yet they were firm.

As Athena looked back at the little men then at the desert beyond, she couldn't say she wasn't happy to be leaving this sandpit of a planet.

When they boarded, the ship was brightly lit and Athena blinked as her eyes adjusted to the intensity of the light.

"Kyro. Lights, please," Xul said, shading his eyes.

"Oh, yes, yes. Sorry about that." A tall bald-headed alien brushed past them as the door closed, and went over to the control panel. The lights soon dimmed to regular intensity and Athena was able to see inside of the ship better.

As Xul led her further inside, he began talking to the tall bald-headed alien about the mission but Athena soon tuned out, her eyes roving around the ship.

There were gadgets everywhere, hanging all over the walls.

Some looked like guns, some were spears, some were intricately designed knives.

In one corner, was more gear. Shields. Vests. Protective hats. Boots.

"I'm Kyro," someone said from behind her and Athena spun, her neck craning upward to meet the face of the one who'd spoken.

A thin hand was outstretched toward her and Athena took it warily. The handshake was equally light.

"Athena."

Xul approached and pulled her into his side.

Kyro's large eyes followed the movement and she was sure that if he had eyebrows, he would have raised them.

"Is the Elysium cloaked?" Xul asked.

"Of course, it is." Kyro turned to him and frowned slightly. "We are ready as soon as the time predetermined arrives."

Xul nodded and motioned toward a section of the ship.

"We will rest and move tomorrow, then. Will you be okay piloting us back into space?"

Kyro nodded. "And what about the human?"

Xul glanced at Athena, then back at Kyro. "She is mine. I am responsible for her safety."

Kyro nodded again. "We will launch in twenty minutes," he said.

With that, Xul spun with her and headed down a section of the ship.

Athena held onto the arm that surrounded her and looked up at him as they walked, frowning.

"What is it, Athena?"

"Who told you that I am yours?" she whispered as they walked into a room that had fluffy pillows on a bed and what looked like a tall shower along the wall.

Xul stalked directly to the shower area and pinned her body against the wall, his eyes burning into hers.

"I showed you before," he spoke, his voice so low, her ears strained to pick up his words.

"Maybe I need to show you again."

24

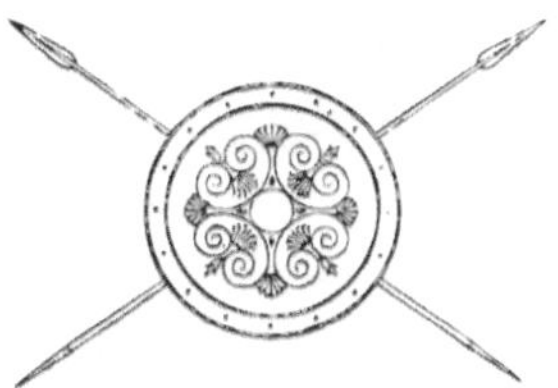

Xul tore off the zehmip coat that was wrapped around her body with one swift movement. He thought she'd be surprised but her mouth slammed into his with as much fervor as he was trying to contain within himself.

Moaning as his body pressed into hers, he felt as she pulled against his loincloth, uttering a frustrated sound when she was not able to remove it.

As he pulled the loincloth off and it fell to the floor, his manhood sprung up between them and he heard her moan into his mouth.

Pressing the button behind her, a warm spray showered down on them and she paused kissing him to raise her face to the falling water.

Xul smiled, reveling in the joy on her face.

He knew she'd have appreciated the shower. It was why it was the first thing he'd headed for once boarding the ship.

Hell, he was enjoying it too.

Showering was usually a monotonous job. Soap, rub, wash. But with Athena's body pressed against his, the water running down his hair and his shoulders, he could appreciate the shower a lot more.

Picking up one of the biola seeds from the tray in the shower, he rubbed it in his hands and smoothed the lather into her hair.

"Mmm," Athena moaned, closing her eyes as she inhaled deeply. "It smells like jasmine."

"I do not know what that is, but I like the smell on you."

Dipping his head to her lips, he sucked her bottom lip into his mouth as the water rinsed the lather from her hair.

He paused for a second when he felt her small hands in his own hair. She'd done the same thing, taking one of the seeds, creating a lather, and was slowly massaging his scalp.

A low rumble of a moan vibrated in his chest and Athena's eyes opened slightly before Xul's mouth crashed into hers again.

Taking another seed in his hand, he created a lather over her shoulders and down her back, moving in slow circles till he reached the curve of her buttocks. Clasping her cheeks, he pulled her into him as his tongue continued to ravage her mouth.

She was so smooth, and soft, and perfect; yet, she was brave, and fearless...a fighter.

"I'll never forget what you did out there," he groaned and then she suddenly froze.

"Is that why you're acting like this?" She looked up at him, her eyes searching his. "Do you think you owe me something?"

"I owe you everything."

"And I, you."

"But that is not why I'm grabbing your ass and pulling you into me, making you feel every inch of the hardness I want to bury inside your warmth."

Athena blinked a few times. "You have a way with words."

It was his turn to blink. "I'm doing this because, despite how I try to ignore it, you are here." He touched his head. "And now also here." He touched his heart and Athena's eyes widened.

Whoa.

But as his mouth crashed into hers again, she knew he was right.

She didn't want to admit it, but that was what was happening to her too.

She'd felt it clearly when she'd seen him lying unresponsive in the sand.

She hadn't wanted to lose him then. And she wasn't sure if she ever wanted to lose him.

Returning his bruising kiss, she gasped as Xul lifted her above his waist, prompting her to wrap her hands around his neck.

His fingers found her folds and he clasped her there, rubbing his finger against her clit as he took one of her nipples into his mouth.

Athena gasped again, her head swinging back as Xul began to draw circles around the throbbing buds—his tongue mimicking the motion his finger was tracing around her clit.

"Oh God. Please..." she begged.

She could feel the thickness of his mushroom brush against her and her pussy throbbed in response.

Wrapping her legs tight around his torso, Athena inhaled deeply as he pushed past her folds.

"Oh shit," she groaned, holding on to him tighter as he pushed past that first bit of resistance and his head popped in.

A moan shuddered through him as he gripped her ass.

She could feel the power in his arms and it was evident he was trying hard to restrain himself so he didn't slam all the way into her too fast and too hard.

But as she clenched around him, Athena opened her eyes.

His cock head felt glorious. So fucking thick. She could almost feel the moisture running down her walls at the thought of it spreading her wide.

Raising her hands to grab onto his horns, she held on tight as she lowered herself onto him slowly.

Xul groaned, breaking the kiss to scorch her with the need in his eyes and Athena's eyes fluttered back in her head.

His cock felt like a ribbed condom and even though she wasn't riding him yet, she could feel the orgasm building deep within her.

She was going to come, and she was going to come hard.

With a grunt, Xul pressed her back against the shower wall and held her there.

His thrusts began slow, spreading her lips wide as he stretched her, then picked up in pace.

Her entire body was vibrating against the cool stone and Athena screamed his name, biting down hard into his shoulder as her orgasm rocked through her. But Xul wasn't done yet.

He pummeled into her, his cock pulling out almost completely till he sheathed himself full hilt within her with thrust after powerful thrust.

It felt like there was honey between her legs as he pumped into her, riding out her climax till she collapsed against him.

As she leaned down and sucked on his neck, Xul grabbed her hands and pinned her back against the shower. The spray was still raining down on them and he was looking her in the eyes.

With each thrust, his gaze seemed to become more intense.

"You are my Athena," he said. "I will protect you with my life."

As his lips crashed down on hers again, she felt him shudder within her, his cock jerking as it released its load.

Xul broke the kiss to stare into her eyes, the mist surrounding them.

"I mean it," he breathed.

And the look in his eyes told her he did.

FOR THE REMAINDER of the evening, Xul discussed battle plans with Kyro, finalizing their tactics while Athena paced.

Tomorrow was the day. She was going to wake up, head out on a ship, and try to get the other females rescued.

Glancing at herself through one of the reflective panels on the ship, she smoothed down the tunic Xul had found for her to wear.

It felt good to have showered and to be wearing clothes for once.

She was still without underwear but that seemed to be a luxury outside of Earth.

Glancing over at Xul, who was sitting around a small table going over the mission with Kyro, Athena exhaled slowly.

He still had not briefed her about her potential role in any part of the plan.

She didn't want to come off as impatient but if she was to be of any assistance tomorrow, she needed to know what was happening.

Walking up behind him, she placed a hand on his shoulder and he glanced at her and smiled.

Damn, he was handsome. She didn't know why she'd been fighting it for so long.

He was handsome. End of.

Yes, his horns reminded her of the devil and of a bull, but damn if he wasn't a handsome devil...no pun intended.

Pointing to the markings they had on the table in front of them, Athena asked, "Where do I fit in all this?"

Xul passed a glance at Kyro before focusing on the plans again.

"Your role is to stay here, on the ship, where it is safe."

Athena cocked her head to the side. She was sure she hadn't heard correctly.

"There is no way I am staying on this ship while I can be of some help out there." She tried to keep her voice level but she was already gritting her teeth.

"It is the best thing for the mission," Xul said, but he didn't look at her.

"Bullshit."

"I don't know that word."

"It means you're talking nonsense."

Slight amusement graced his features and Kyro was looking at her as if he was raising his eyebrows again, if he did have any.

"You stay here on the ship." Xul finally looked at her. "It's the only way I will know you're safe."

"I'm sure you'd appreciate it if I was fighting by your side. I may not be good with fancy weapons but I think on my feet."

"Bullshit," Xul said, and Athena raised an eyebrow. "To the first part. I do not want you fighting by my side. I don't want to see you fighting for your life. Not again. Not so soon."

She could feel the meaning behind his words and understood him completely.

That fight they'd had where the Isclit and the gator-guards had come searching for them, it was still burned into her mind too.

Death had been so close and she'd brushed hands with it.

It hadn't been a good feeling and it was one she didn't want to experience again anytime soon.

But that didn't stop the fact that she needed to go onboard to help the only link she had back to Earth.

Those women, Diana, Piper, Evren, and Song...they were literally the only humans she would ever see again in her lifetime.

If she could have done something to help them escape and she didn't, she would never forgive herself.

Xul seemed to read her thoughts as he studied her and he was already shaking his head as he looked at her.

"I don't like it," he said.

"Well, it isn't what you like. It's what I need to do."

Xul's mouth set into a hard line and his eyes flared. But she didn't care if he was going to get into a hissy fit about it.

Her mind was already made up.

"I have to do this. They are the only humans I have."

Turning back to the plans on the table, Xul seemed to contemplate things for a second while Kyro silently studied them both.

Without a word, Xul pulled her onto his lap and pressed his face into her hair.

"I just discovered you," he said. "I don't want to lose you."

Again, it seemed as if Kyro was raising his nonexistent eyebrows.

She guessed it was strange to see or hear Xul say such things.

Kyro cocked his head to the side and studied her.

"Your species bewitches," he whispered.

Athena gave him a look and Xul chuckled.

"Yes," he said. "She's cast some sort of spell over me." Leaning back in the chair, Xul regarded her with narrowed eyes.

"Fine. You come with me. But you listen to everything I say." He paused. "Even if it means leaving me behind."

From the look in his eyes, she knew he was thinking about the last time she was supposed to leave him behind.

Athena shook her head immediately.

"Only if you promise you'll do the same for me."

25

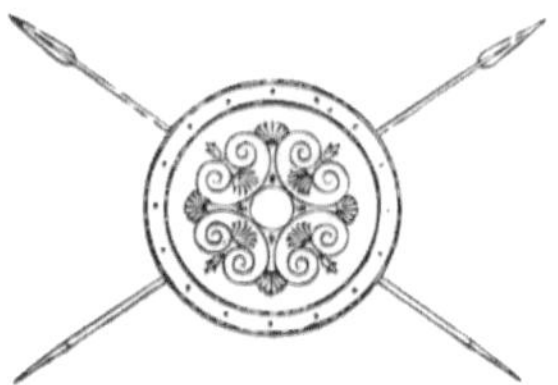

Athena spun in the reinforced skin-tight outfit Xul had given her to put on.

The thing covered her like a Catwoman suit but it was deceivingly comfortable.

"It is resistant to most pierce attacks, poison, and acid," he said, his gaze roving over her form appreciatively.

As they walked into the weapons closet, Xul grabbed another version of his spear. This one had a bigger blade than the last and was covered in strange inscriptions.

As Athena looked around, her eyes fell on what looked like a gun the size of a small hairdryer.

It had round red bumps all along the top and Athena reached for it tentatively.

"That's the sidr," Xul said, walking over to her. "It homes in on your target. Attaches to their body, then detonates like a grenade."

Athena raised her eyebrows. She hated guns, mostly because she had terrible aim, but this sounded like the right weapon for her.

"You just try to aim in the direction of your target. It will home in on the nearest enemy. The genetic codes of the Tasqals and their men have already been coded into the weapon," Xul continued.

Ooh, even better.

Grabbing the gun, she slipped it in the waistband of the suit and reached for a curved dagger.

"That dagger is incredibly sharp and incredibly dangerous," Xul warned.

"Just the way it's supposed to be." Athena smiled, sheathing the dagger and placing it on the other side of her waist.

Kyro shuffled into the room then, his gaze on Athena before he turned to Xul.

"We are in view of the Isclit ship, Commander," he said.

Athena glanced at Xul.

Commander.

She liked the sound of that.

"Is the ship ready?"

"It is."

"The bombs?"

Kyro nodded. "Already loaded in the ship."

"And the distorters?"

Kyro outstretched his hand with what looked like two watches on them.

Xul took them both and slipped one over his wrist before passing the other to her.

"What are these?"

Xul smiled. "I'll show you."

Pressing the button on the side of the watch, his entire body morphed into that of a gator-guard almost immediately.

Athena jumped back. "What the fuck?!"

"It is still me." Xul's voice sounded weird coming from the mouth of the thing. "It is old technology but it will work for what we need it to do."

Athena's eyes widened as he pressed the button on his watch and returned to his usual form.

Old technology?

Even the biggest technology firms on Earth weren't even close to creating something like that.

Securing the watch over her wrist, Athena pressed the button.

In the next second, her body was morphed into that of an Isclit.

"Fuck me..." she murmured.

Xul cleared his throat. "Oh, I want to...but not in that form."

Trying not to smile, Athena narrowed her eyes at him and was glad the Isclit's eyes communicated that emotion quite perfectly.

"Our weapons and everything we carry are hidden while we are using the distorters," Xul said. "That means, if we need to use our weapons, we cannot be distorted."

Athena nodded, pressing the button again to return to her usual form.

"It is time." Kyro's voice reached their ears and Xul locked eyes with her once more before he nodded and led the way down a small corridor.

As they exited into a larger room, Athena saw a ship that was identical to the one they'd crashed onto Muk in.

Her heart hammered in her chest at the memory and she glanced at Xul.

"The other one was rigged," he said. "We were supposed to crash." Then a thoughtful look crossed over his face. "I wouldn't dare put your life in danger like that again."

Athena nodded.

It didn't matter anyway. Even if he didn't want to think about it, he didn't have a choice.

She was going with him even if it meant crash-landing on some other planet again.

This was a war she had to fight. A war she hadn't asked to be a part of but one in which she played a vital role, nonetheless.

The other women were counting on her.

She wouldn't let them down.

As the butterfly doors of the small ship opened, Athena climbed into the passenger seat and buckled herself in, glancing back at Kyro as Xul entered the pilot's seat.

"He isn't coming?"

"No, he has to guard the Elysium till we return. The only way he will come is if something goes wrong."

Athena turned to face forward and exhaled a deep breath.

"Well then," she breathed. "Let's hope that nothing goes wrong."

As the ship's engine began to hum and the vessel rose into the air, Kyro went back into the ship and sealed the door shut.

Next, the larger doors in front of them were opening and the little ship shot forward.

Xul placed a hand over hers, as he studied her face.

"Are you sure this is what you want to do?" he asked.

"Positive."

She'd forgotten how big the Isclit ship was.

Seeing it again was a bit jarring.

Glancing at Xul, she noticed his face was set into a hard expression. She'd seen that look before when they'd been trekking through the desert on Muk.

Funny, that felt like so long ago now.

"You still haven't told me exactly what I'm supposed to do once we get on that ship..."

Xul glanced at her for a second before averting his gaze.

"You will stay by my side until we can free your friends."

"That's all? You mentioned bombs."

"I have to set the charges. They'll detonate once we have everyone off the ship."

Athena nodded. It seemed simple enough.

Looking ahead, she realized they were now quite close to the Isclit ship.

"We have to distort ourselves now," Xul said, glancing at her.

Athena nodded again and took a deep breath, pressing the button on her watch.

It was almost as if she could feel her body shrink as she settled into the form of an Isclit.

When she looked beside her again, Xul was gazing back at her in the body of a gator-guard.

"That's so creepy…"

Xul seemed to smile, then his face got serious.

They were right next to the ship now and a sound came over the intercom.

"Ship 5869. State your business." It sounded like a gator-guard.

"Returning from a meeting with the High Tasqal Mercurion," Xul stated.

For a few seconds, there was no reply and Athena found she was holding her breath.

"Cleared. Enter at Gate 12V4."

Xul switched off the intercom and glanced at her as the large doors of the ship opened in front of them.

"Good job, Yce," he murmured.

Ah, so it appeared Yce was working behind the scenes so this all went smoothly.

The fact that this was a serious operation was not lost on her.

As they entered the ship, Athena took a deep breath.

It looked just like the cargo bay she'd seen when she'd left the ship the last time. Only, now, there were no aliens waiting to be transported and there was no hustle and bustle.

Apart from the few gator-guards guarding the area, there was not much happening.

Maybe that was for the best.

As Xul docked the spacecraft, he glanced at her.

"Here, use this," he said, handing her a glowing light-blue ring as his now-yellow eyes regarded her.

Oh, yes.

She'd completely forgotten that the Isclits only seemed to travel around on these things.

"It will move in any direction you put your weight. The speed depends on how hard you press down."

Simple enough.

As the doors of the ship opened, Athena placed the ring underneath her feet and stood shakily.

As her weight settled on the thing, it began to hover lightly above the ground.

She was bending down over the other side of the ship, trying to get her bearings, when she heard a gator-guard approach them.

"Soldier, you are stationed on this ship?" the gator-guard asked as he approached. He was addressing Xul. Apparently, he hadn't seen her on the other side of the ship.

Xul didn't answer and Athena's heart suddenly began to race.

If he spoke, there was a good chance that they would be found out.

He didn't sound anything like a gator-guard. They all sounded the same, as if they were cloned.

"You dare not answer your commander?" She could hear the gator-guard's rising anger.

She needed to do something.

Now.

Hovering around the side of the ship, she narrowed her eyes, hoping the Isclit's eyes were doing the same thing effectively.

She could see Xul's eyes widen slightly when he saw her and she could see mild surprise in the real gator-guard's features.

"The guard's. Station. Is none. Of your. Business," Athena said, trying as best as she could to keep her voice monotone. "Get back. To your. Position."

The gator-guard paused for a second before he mumbled an apology and walked away.

As soon as he was out of earshot, Xul seemed to smile.

"Quick thinking, little human."

Athena narrowed her eyes some more and smiled.

Xul frowned. "Don't do that."

A glance at her reflection and Athena almost cringed. Isclit faces weren't meant for smiling.

The line that was her mouth looked all squiggly as if it was having a hard time forcing itself upward. It was probably why none of them ever smiled.

"Let's go," Xul said, glancing behind them as they walked through a door.

"Wait," Athena whispered, as they entered a corridor. "Shouldn't I be in front of you? I never see the Isclit's walking behind the guards."

Xul paused and glanced back at her. "But you don't know where to go."

"You will just have to direct me then." Athena hovered in front of him and even with the face of the gator-guard, she could see he was somewhat amused.

As they walked down the corridor, she heard Xul murmur "left" behind her.

Taking the next left, they came upon another corridor.

"Fifth door down," Xul whispered and Athena paused walking as she glanced back at him.

"Doors? There are no doors."

Xul's eyes narrowed. "Right. The ship is programmed to acknowledge only certain lifeforms. To you, there are no doors or other exits. For me, they are visible."

It was all clear.

That was why she hadn't been able to figure out how they were opening the doors before.

"Maybe you should walk beside me then."

Xul narrowed his eyes as they began walking again, moving to her side.

"Here," he breathed, pausing before the wall.

Shortly after, a door appeared and they stepped into a dark room.

There were pipes networking along the walls for as far as she could see.

As soon as the door closed behind them, Xul pressed the button on his watch and returned to his usual form.

"There are no cameras here. We are safe."

Taking his lead, Athena did the same and stepped off the light-blue ring. She'd just have to carry it in her hand for now.

The room was dark, with little white lights dotting the floor.

"What is this place?" she asked as they began moving.

"It's the belly of the ship. This leads down to the engine."

As he spoke, he was placing some little disks along the wall after every few steps.

"The bombs," he answered her unasked question.

Athena nodded, glancing behind her.

It was dark.

So dark.

Apart from the lights on the ground, she couldn't see anything. She was just about to turn around when she was sure she saw something move in the darkness behind them.

Pausing for a few seconds, she strained her eyes to see but there was nothing there. All that was behind them was darkness.

Inching forward, she followed the glowing lights that dotted the path ahead.

Every few seconds, she could hear Xul attach another bomb to the wall. Going by how far they'd walked, he'd attached at least ten of the things so far. She wondered if it would be enough to take down the massive ship.

She was just about to ask him about it when she bumped into his chest.

"Xu—"

His finger covered her lips and silenced her.

With a sniff, he smelled the air, and Athena stiffened.

He'd sensed something. Even through the darkness, she could see enough to know that his eyes were narrowed.

Pulling her into him, he peered into the darkness.

Maybe she had seen something move in the darkness behind them.

Pressing her against the wall, Xul whispered to her that she shouldn't move.

Athena nodded, their gazes locking before Xul eased off her and headed back the way they came.

She was waiting for what felt like the longest minute before she heard something hit against the pipes.

A roar echoed within the space that made her heart rate accelerate. It didn't sound like Xul.

It was something else.

A gator-guard.

That meant they definitely weren't alone.

As Athena craned her ears, the undeniable sound of something big and heavy rushing her way caught her ears.

Eyes wide, Athena grabbed the gun at her waist and aimed.

26

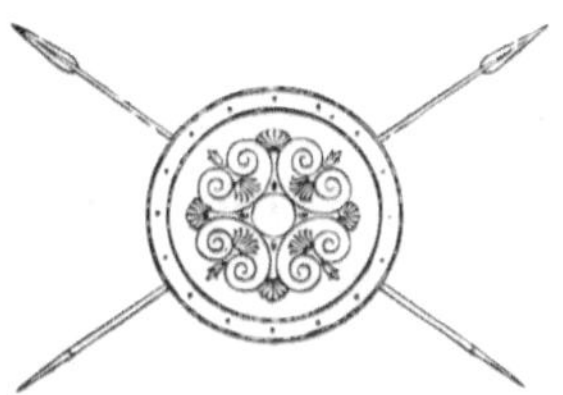

Xul appeared before her suddenly and Athena released a breath.

"We were followed by that guard from the dock," he said, breathless. "We have to hurry. I have no idea if he set off an alarm."

He was already leading the way, adding bombs as they ran along the length of the space till they reached the end and another door suddenly appeared in the wall.

"Distorter," Xul breathed, as he stepped out of the space.

Pressing the button on her watch, Athena stepped on the lightblue hover ring she'd been carrying and hovered out of the darkness.

This section looked familiar and excitement built in her chest as her pulse drummed in her ears. They were on the floor where the cells were located.

But there was another noise as well—heavy footsteps running down the corridor toward them.

Turning in the other direction, Xul set off on a run and Athena hovered behind him.

When he reached one of the cells, he glanced inside then moved to another.

He did this for a few more, all the while the sound of footsteps behind them approaching fast.

When he finally stopped in front of one of the cells, he distorted to his usual form and slashed the cell with his spear.

The bars crumpled as if the blade was made of acid.

"Crex," Xul said, his eyes widening as an alien appeared from the cell.

The two nodded to each other and Athena remembered the name immediately.

This was the member of his team who had bonded.

As she reached the cell and the two turned to face her, Crex snarled as he crouched to attack.

Xul placed a hand on the alien's shoulder. "No, brother. She is with us."

"She?" Athena heard Crex ask as he narrowed his eyes at her.

Just then, a set of gator-guards, maybe seven or so of them, turned the corner, weapons poised.

Xul nodded to Crex just as Athena pressed the button on her distorter so she could take out the gun.

But Crex was already launching himself through the air.

He was fast. Just a blur as he jumped past Athena, balancing along the walls as he headed straight towards the guards.

She only had a moment to widen her eyes before she heard a familiar voice.

"Athena?"

Spinning her head, Athena peered into the dim cell.

Rainbow colored hair framed a face that was looking back at her.

"Piper?!" Athena choked.

"Oh my God, I thought you were dead!" Piper crashed into her, holding her close.

Athena couldn't say anything. The emotions were too strong.

She'd seen and experienced so many strange things since being taken from Earth that every little contact she'd had with humans since then was something to be cherished.

Through the corner of her eye, she saw Xul moving down the corridor, swiftly slicing through the cages.

Just then, to her other side, a loud growl echoed from Crex as he took out one of the guards who was rushing their way.

From the opposite direction, she heard more footsteps approaching and an alarm was now blaring loudly through the ship.

Pulling away from Piper's embrace, she held the woman's face and looked her in the eyes.

"Get the others," she said, glancing back at Crex.

Somehow, he had managed to take out five of the guards on his own but now one had its teeth sunk deep into his back while the other was lifting a jagged knife to plunge into his chest.

With a war cry she didn't even know she had, Athena pulled the gun from her waist, as she rushed toward them.

Falling on one knee, she aimed and pressed the trigger.

Small red dots burst from the gun and landed on the gator-guard's back, sinking into the alien's thick skin.

The guard roared and turned to her, its eyes furious as it stalked toward her.

Crex managed to pull the other off his shoulder and in one swift move, he wrapped his hands around its neck and twisted, rendering the beast immobile.

The other was still stalking toward her and Athena fired again.

Another burst of red dots shot from the gun and embedded themselves in the guard's skin. As the guard aimed the knife at her, it suddenly stopped as it locked eyes with her gun and then with her.

In that moment, it was as if realization hit as its eyes noticeably widened.

In the next second, its body split into pieces as if it was blown apart from the inside.

Athena glanced at the gun with wide eyes.

Damn.

When she looked up, Crex was standing above her.

"Thank you," he said, his eyes still narrowed as he regarded her. His shoulder was covered in blood but he didn't seem to even notice.

As his eyes averted to something behind her, Athena turned to realize that the corridor was now filled with aliens, and, among them, the women from Earth.

Xul and two other aliens were busy fighting the guards who had approached, taking them all out easily.

"Let's go," Crex said, brushing past her.

Athena was on her feet, running behind him as they reached the group.

As Xul turned and saw her, he pushed through the crowd to pull her into his arms, burying his face in her neck.

"Don't do that again," he breathed.

"Don't do what?"

"My men can handle themselves."

"So can I."

He raised his head to look at her then and she saw the worry leave his eyes slowly.

"So you can," he murmured.

Someone cleared their throat and a light-blue alien approached from the group. On his forehead, what looked like a large gem was embedded in his skin.

"We must move," he said, his eyes locking with Athena's. "More guards are on their way."

As she looked at him, she felt a strange fuzzy feeling in her mind.

"Yce, she is mine. You are not allowed in her mind," Xul said.

Immediately, the fuzzy feeling went away and Yce pulled his gaze from hers.

"Athena!" It was Diana. Her red hair was tangled and she looked dirty as hell, but she was smiling nonetheless.

Behind her, all the other women were greeting each other and Athena looked up at Xul.

He nodded, obviously knowing what she needed to do.

Approaching the women with wide arms, they shared a brief embrace.

They were all there: Piper, Song, Diana, and Evren.

The sight of them all safe and together made her heart swell with joy.

More shouting was heard down the corridor and they all glanced at the aliens around them.

"This way," said the one with the gem in his forehead.

Rushing down the corridor, they soon came upon a wall.

Xul stepped in front of it and a door opened, leading them into a loading dock with several ships.

Several ships and many, many guards.

It only took a second for realization to pass between the two groups before weapons were drawn.

Pulling out her gun, Athena began shooting. By her side, she heard Piper scream as she dashed toward one of the guards, bare-handed, only to be taken down from the side by Crex.

Hoisting Piper over his shoulder, Crex grabbed one of the guards by the snout and squeezed so hard the guard's snout crumpled.

As her bullets hit one of the guards heading toward her and the guard exploded, she saw Xul dash in front, his spear moving through the air beautifully as he sliced through guard after guard.

To his left, Song was...flying?

She was on the back of an alien Athena hadn't seen before and he was literally soaring over them all as he headed to a ship on the far side of the dock.

To her right, Diana and Evren were both attacking one guard together.

"Catch!" she shouted as she pulled the dagger she was carrying from her waist and threw it in their direction.

Diana caught the thing like a pro and didn't hesitate to bury the blade in the gator-guard's eye.

It was chaos.

Beautiful chaos and Athena never felt more alive.

If she had thought that she'd ever be doing something like this, she would have laughed at the idea. It wasn't possible, and yet, it was.

She was doing it.

As Xul sliced the last guard's throat, he took a breath and looked around until their eyes locked.

This was so much more than she had ever been able to imagine.

He was so much more.

Suddenly, life on Earth just seemed...bland.

If she could, how would she even be able to go back to living normally after this?

The thought was an exhilarating one, and she smiled at Xul.

Slight amusement lit up his features and something else clouded his eyes as he looked at her.

Pride?

Love?

"We board and head to the Elysium," he said to the others as he approached her.

Again, he pulled her into his arms.

"Let's go, little human."

Athena smiled.

"Ok, my big alien."

Xul grinned back.

27

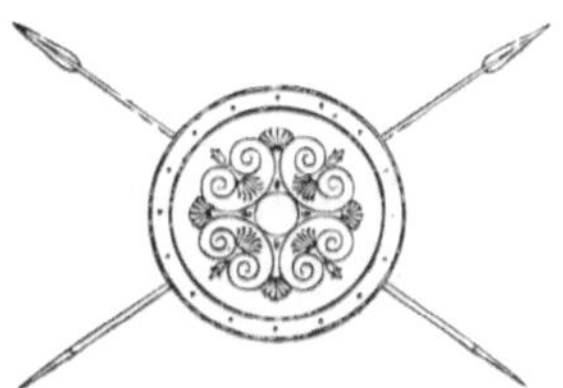

As they zoomed out of the Isclit ship Athena turned her head to look back. They were only just safely enough away before she saw a large explosion rip through the center of the ship. Then it was like a chain reaction.

That explosion triggered another, and another, and soon the once imposing ship was being ripped apart.

"The Mukkians will be happy with this," Xul mused, a soft smile on his face.

"What do you mean?"

"Most of the debris will fall on their world. They trade metal scraps for wares."

Well, that explained why they so happily gathered the ship they'd taken down after the Isclits had come looking for her.

"So, did you do it?"

Xul glanced at her then and stretched his hand across to brush a finger against her cheek.

"We did it," he said.

As space lit up behind them, Athena released a breath she hadn't realized she'd been holding. But she couldn't help but feel somewhat unsettled in her stomach.

"It's a huge ship," she said. "Just how many innocent beings did we just have to destroy to take it down?"

Xul glanced at her, noting the concern in her eyes. "When the ship visited your planet, it had just begun its journey. The plan was to gather more slaves. That won't happen now."

So it was over.

The nightmare was over.

The Isclits were gone and there was no way for them to recapture her.

She was free.

As they approached the Elysium and docked, she watched as the other aliens hopped out of the ships and headed inside.

Xul hopped out and came around to her side to lift her down and, as they headed inside the Elysium, she realized he didn't let go of her hand.

Once inside, there were greetings going around.

"We made it," Song breathed, as she smiled at the other women. The alien with the wings was standing close by, an arm draped around Song's waist.

Beside them, Piper was standing and Athena was just able to really look at her properly.

Piper was dressed in a blanket that was wrapped around her haphazardly and so were the others. But unlike the others, Piper had deep welts on her back. As Athena stared, the women turned their heads and saw her looking.

"Athena!" Evren shouted, a grin on her face. "Or should we say, Cat Woman?"

Athena smiled, pulling her eyes away from Piper's wounds.

"I'm so happy you all are okay."

"You look more than okay. Looks like you ended up with the right alien." Diana glanced at Xul, who was standing with his men, supposedly having a meeting but his gaze was in their direction, or rather, on Athena.

"Looks like it," Athena breathed, as her eyes drifted to Crex.

His back was turned to her and, with all the commotion she

hadn't noticed it before, but his back was filled with the same deep grooves that were on Piper.

If her memory served her right, he was the Ceqtaq. The same vicious species the High Tasqals had been talking about. And if his fighting was anything to go by, he was vicious indeed.

Athena frowned as she glanced back at Piper, finally taking in the woman's bloodied lip.

"Oh my God, Piper," she whispered, moving closer to the woman. "Did he hurt you?"

Piper frowned. "Who?"

"The one you were imprisoned with."

Realization seemed to flood over Piper's eyes as she shook her head, glancing Crex's way.

As if the alien was listening to them, he stalked over, and lifted Piper over his shoulder.

Piper's squeal did nothing to stop him and the other women could only open their eyes wide as they watched him march away down the corridor to one of the rooms.

Just then, Kyro approached, his gaze also following Crex.

"Interesting," he murmured before turning to the women. "Human women. We are about to leave this section of space. For safety, you must all be strapped in."

Athena nodded, taking a step toward the seats when she too was suddenly lifted off her feet and thrown over someone's shoulder.

"Xul!" She hit him on his back as a deep flush colored her cheeks.

She could imagine what the other women were thinking and was only happy she couldn't see their faces.

"I will make sure she is strapped down, Kyro," Xul said, marching off with her.

"Strapped in..." Kyro corrected, lifting a finger.

"I think he meant exactly what he said." Athena heard one of the other aliens comment.

Xul threw her on the bed as he climbed on top of her.

"What about the others? I haven't had a chance to speak with them yet." Athena giggled as Xul nibbled on her ear.

"They can wait."

His eyes were full of need as he ripped at the suit impatiently.

When she was finally naked in front of him, he drank her in.

"My little human," he breathed, dipping his head to her breast.

"My big alien," Athena gasped at the sudden warmth of his mouth.

Rolling her nipple underneath his tongue, he moved off her breast and traced a path down to her navel.

He paused there to take her hips between his hands as he buried his face in her center.

"You're mine," he said, and a thrill went up her spine as he kissed her there.

"I need you," she murmured, writhing her hips against him. She needed to feel him, needed to be taken to ecstasy by the feel of him within her.

"So soon?" Xul lifted his head and Athena looked down at him with hooded eyes. She could already tell, without even touching herself, that she was dripping wet down there.

"I need you now," she said again, her voice hoarse with need.

She watched as it seemed like a fire lit up his eyes as he rose above her and settled between her legs.

"Open for me, Athena," Xul breathed into her ear and she willingly obliged, spreading her legs as she felt his thick mushroom tip press against her entrance.

As he pressed past that first bit of resistance, Athena moaned loudly. She didn't know if she would ever get used to it, but his thickness felt so darn good and, judging from the rumble of pleasure emanating from his chest, he enjoyed the feeling too.

Xul began thrusting slowly, raising his head to gaze into her eyes, his green becoming more intense with every thrust.

It was so intimate, just the two of them, connected at some spot in space, and Athena could feel the sweet nectar of an orgasm building deep within her.

It was only him.

He was hers and she was his.

It felt perfect.

It felt right.

And as Xul slid deep within her, Athena held his gaze as her orgasm flowed through her core.

"Xul," she breathed. She could feel herself clenching against him and watched as he gritted his teeth.

He was going to reach his peak and she held his face between her hands.

"I am yours," she whispered, as his orgasm pulsed through him.

When his manhood finally stopped jerking and he rested beside her, Xul pulled her into his arms.

"If I had known you were on the other side of the universe all this time, I would have come and abducted you myself," he said, planting a kiss underneath her ear.

Athena smiled.

They lay together in silence as she felt the ship suddenly pick up speed.

They were leaving this section of space to go to another. One with more adventures and more aliens and more worlds. Things she would have never even been able to imagine before.

"Athena..." Xul murmured.

"Yes?"

"If there was a way for you to go back to your home planet," he said. "Would you take it?"

Athena took a few moments to think about it.

What was there for her on Earth? Even if she did manage to go back, how would she even be able to live a normal life after all this?

"Are you saying there is a way?" She turned to him slightly.

"No. But if there was?"

Athena released a sigh.

"If there was, I don't think I'd take it."

"Why is that?"

"If I took it, I'd have to leave everything behind. All of this. Everything I know now. These last few days have been the worst and best days of my life."

"Have they?"

"Yes. And if I left, I'd have to leave you."

Xul frowned. "I could come with you. Do they not have any creatures that look like me on your planet?"

Athena let out a laugh.

"A bit but it's not the same."

"So you will stay with me then?"

Turning to him fully, Athena looked into his deep green eyes.

"Always." She smiled then added, "As long as you always stay with me, too, my big alien."

"Always." Xul pulled her towards him and planted his lips against hers.

"Always, my little human."

ALSO BY AG WILDE

Xul: Captured by Aliens Book One
Athena wakes up in hell.
Well…it's an alien slave ship, but it might as well be hell because she only has three choices.
Mate. Become a sex slave. Or be killed.
Great options.
Desperate for freedom, a chance for survival is presented in the handsome rogue alien called Xul.
But Xul is caught up in problems of his own and a mission he cannot afford to let fail—one that could be easily compromised if he dared open his heart.
That doesn't leave her with many options and it doesn't help that she finds him utterly frustrating...
...and strong, hot, irresistible...
She shouldn't really be thinking about him like that. Should she?

Other books in the series: Crex, Yce, Kyris, Kyro

Riv's Sanctuary: Riv's Sanctuary Book One
Abducted from Earth over a year ago, Lauren spent most of that time getting accustomed to her new life as one of the "animals" in an alien zoo.

When she's sold by the zookeeper, her life takes a turn she wasn't expecting. She has no idea where she'll end up till she's brought to a sanctuary owned by a tall blue hunk of an alien called Riv.

Riv's life is quiet and peaceful in a place as far away from civilization as he can manage. So when an annoying chatterbox of a human ends up on his doorstep, he's less than pleased. The human disrupts his life and his solitude and he can't wait to get rid of her.

He's not interested in helping her, and he's definitely not interested in love.

Except...she's managed to wheedle her way in and suddenly those barriers around his heart don't seem so strong anymore.

He has two options: Let her go.

Or let her in.

Other books in the series: Sohut's Protection, Ka'Cit's Haven

—

Ajos: The Restitution Book One
She didn't move to the big city just to be kidnapped by aliens.
That wasn't even possible...
Right?
WRONG.
When Kerena wakes up, she's not on Earth anymore.
Heck, she's not even in the same galaxy, and the face hovering so close she can make out every detail? That face is definitely...not...human.
But before she can really figure out what's going on, Kerena realizes she's caught in the middle of a war—one she was thrust into as soon as she was ripped from Earth.
She's surrounded by aliens in a rebellion, but there's one—the one with the strange golden eyes, minty-teal skin, and rippling muscles—that holds her attention.
His presence is magnetic and his heated gaze makes something stir deep within her.
He's battling something that has nothing to do with the war and his warning that she should stay away does not go unheeded.

He's a dangerous rebel fighter. She gets that. So...why is he still hovering so close? And why is he growling at everyone that so much as looks in her direction?

Most of all, why does he keep looking at her like she belongs to ... HIM?

Other books in the series: V'Alen

—

Arrival: Captured Earth Book One

ADIRA
The machines came, and they trampled us all.
I have nothing left. No family. No friends. No home.
They harvest us. They breed us. They feed from us...
There is no hope...Not until one fateful moment when my eyes open and I see something streaking across the skies.
What appears is like a demon before my eyes...
But can they be worse than the evil already upon us?
I will just have to wait and see.

FER'RO
Sailing across the stars for what feels like eons...we have followed our enemy to a little blue planet.
We had wanted to arrive before them...now I think we may be too late.
But when we kill the first Scrit and I see the being drowning within its depths, I know I have to save it.
And *it*...turns out to be a *her*. **A female.**
This planet has hope yet. I will save her and her kind.
...Little do I know...she's the one who ends up saving me instead.

Dark. Steamy. Gritty. A thrilling romance intertwined in a plot that will give you chills.

Other books in the series: Base Zero, Cataclysm, War

—

Claiming His Mate
Fated Mates of the Atari

When I get a once-in-a-lifetime chance to go on a luxury space cruise, I jump at it.
This cruise is the beginning of something amazing, and nothing is going to stop me from going.
But when things go wrong shortly after departure, it's clear I have made a mistake.
Suddenly thrown into a world where I have no way of defending myself, the last thing I expect is an Atari warrior coming to my rescue.
This cruise has been full of surprises...but the Atari is the biggest one of all.
He's tall, growly, possessive, and he sends my pulse into overdrive with just the slightest look.
Why the heck is my body reacting this way to this stranger?
And did he just declare that I am his mate?

Other books in the series: Craving His Mate, Fighting for His Mate, Guarding His Mate

—

Scan the QR code to view all books

ABOUT THE AUTHOR

A. G. Wilde is an avid reader, a gamer, a lover of all things space, alien, and sci-fi.

She is addicted to intense romance, irresistible heroes, and deliciously naughty things.

Scan the QR code below if you want to ☞ Join her mailing list, ☞ Find her on Facebook , ☞ or visit her website.

❋☆☼☆❋

 facebook.com/agwilde

twitter.com/authoragwilde

instagram.com/authoragwilde

amazon.com/author/agwilde